Half-Breed

Half-Breed

Scott Michael Decker

Copyright (C) 2014 Scott Michael Decker
Layout Copyright (C) 2015 Creativia

Published 2015 by Creativia
Book sdesign by Creativia (www.creativia.org)
Cover art by http://www.thecovercollection.com/
This book is a work of fiction. Names, characters, places, and incidents are the product of the author's imagination or are used fictitiously. Any resemblance to actual events, locales, or persons, living or dead, is purely coincidental.
All rights reserved. No part of this book may be reproduced or transmitted in any form or by any means, electronic or mechanical, including photocopying, recording, or by any information storage and retrieval system, without the author's permission.
U.S. Copyright application # 1-1784366411

Titles by the Author

If you like this novel, please post a review on the website where you purchased it, and consider other novels from among these titles by Scott Michael Decker:

Science Fiction:
Cube Rube
Doorport
Drink the Water
Edifice Abandoned
Glad You're Born
Half-Breed
Inoculated
Legends of Lemuria
The Gael Gates
War Child

Fantasy:
Bandit and Heir (Series)
Gemstone Wyverns
Sword Scroll Stone

Look for these titles at your favorite e-book retailer.

Chapter 1

"Half-breed!"

Amber Calico spun and slashed at the Felly who'd insulted her, her claws raking through fur and whisker, the tabby cheek sprouting livid red stripes.

The two opponents squared off, the commissary going instantly silent.

She looks as surprised as I feel, Amber thought. She'd just squeezed her hybrid bulk into the narrow checkout lane with that day's groceries, when the pussy had sneered the pejorative at her.

Her thin, calico fur prickled, and a hiss escaped her.

The pussy hissed back and leaped.

Amber ducked and kicked, her opponent twisted mid-air, and the kick sent a shelf tumbling, victuals flying.

She crouched, leapt, slashed, twisted, tumbled, and kicked, Amber holding her own with the smaller, faster opponent, using her greater bone density and weight to advantage. She had fought Felly of similar stature many times, but her opponent had never encountered someone like her. She turned a slash into a throw and hurled the pussy into a coldcase. Glass shattered and bottles scattered. Leaping upon her, she threw triple punches to the ribcage, blocked a slash and dropped a slug to the pussy's jaw.

The other Felly went limp.

A primordial yowl deep in her throat, Amber turned slowly, her brow furrowed.

The line at the register had cleared, and the clerk quickly checked Amber's items, his ears flattened to his skull.

She paid and left, stepping past her unconscious opponent.

Outside, she secured her groceries to her back and dropped to all fours. Burning inside at the insult, she trotted toward home, her right shoulder stiff, the pain masked by adrenaline.

Not Amber's fault her Human father had landed on Felly in the wake of the Terran conquest, Felly the last of many worlds to succumb to the armies of the Terran Emperor Chingis Khan. Not Amber's fault that they'd held the Felly in virtual serfdom, fouling the air and water with their decrepit factories and cesspit mines, hazardous to work in but safer than rebelling. Not Amber's fault that they'd raped and pillaged in victory, leaving behind a traumatized populace, reminded of it for years by hulking halflings like herself.

Livid, she wished she had one of the Terran transpods—the one-person transport vehicles that could take a person across the galaxy in a heartbeat. With transpods, the Terran onslaught had been unstoppable.

Amber trotted toward her street, she and her mother occupying a one-room flat at the back of an eighty-room building. She turned the corner and froze.

A group stood around the building entrance. "There she is!"

Already, she felt them behind her. The banded thugs who carried out the orders of their Terran oppressors. On the upper arm was a silver band etched with a Terran hand, palm out, fingers together, a gesture they'd all been taught that meant "stop."

"Stop. You're under arrest."

Hands grabbed her from behind, and they all joined in to throw her to the ground, more roughly because she was half-Terran.

Amber's one regret was not seeing her mother before they hauled her away.

* * *

"Half-breed!"

Kathy Mongrel whirled on the Canny and thrust her face into his. "You sad excuse for a schnauzer!" She ducked his blow, which shook bibs on the library shelves. "Go on, try that again, you clumsy oaf!" She sidestepped a kick, her smaller form lithe and wiry. "That the best you can do?!" She weaved to the side and his ham-size fist caught a shelf, which exploded in splinters. "You prehistoric throw-back! Microbrain packhound!" And she dodged two blows in rapid succession.

Kathy had been researching microfusion assembly between classes when the Canny had blundered past her and sneered the pejorative at her. Half-Terran, she was smaller than nearly all her full Canny peers, their bulk and brawn no match for her light, fast frame.

"Where's the wolf in you, you drooling, droop-tailed, limp-eared mutt!"

The Canny dropped to all fours and leaped at her.

She rolled to one side, and he crashed into the shelf and fell unconscious, the whole case teetering slowly, and falling into the next, which teetered slowly then fell into the next …

Her face carefully composed, fuming inside at the insult, Kathy walked primly and calmly toward the stairs, descending to the ground floor with nary a look back, heading for the exit across the room. The hue and cry from above reached her.

Not Kathy's fault her Human father had visited in the aftermath of the Canny capitulation to the Terran Emperor Chingis Khan, their race having surrendered to its everlasting chagrin, lest the Terran conquerors ravage the Canny homeplanet as they had nearly every other planet in the Alpha Quadrant. Not

Kathy's fault that their young Canny were conscripted into the Terran armies, their bulk and ferocity making them excellent front-line fodder for further Terran conquest. Not Kathy's fault her mother had fallen in love with a handsome Terran and months later had given birth to this hybrid girl long after the Terran had moved on.

Kathy strode resolutely toward the library door, livid and wishing she had one of the Terran transpods—the one-person transport vehicles that could take a person across the galaxy in a heartbeat. With transpods, the Terran onslaught had been unstoppable. She just wanted one to take her from her miserable existence.

A banded Canny stepped in front of the door, the metal band on his arm etched with a Terran hand, palm out. An Imperial affiliate.

The Traitor! She walked into him as though she didn't see him. Like most of her fellow Cannies, he easily outweighed her, and she bounced harmlessly off him.

"Where ya going? Such a hurry." He had the laconic speech of unhurried authority.

She didn't need to look behind to know she had no escape. "What's it to you, muscle-headed pin-brain?"

A casual smile spread across his droopy jowls, canines glinting between drool-slathered lips.

Disgusting dog! she thought, knowing she looked just as repulsive to him, her thin fur barely concealing her skin.

"Now just come quietly, miss poodle toy, and everything—"

"Don't call me that, bull-face!"

"I didn't start the name callin', but I'd be happy to finish it."

She stared at the barrel of his blaster. I didn't even see him draw it. "What do you want?"

"Just come with me. The Imperials want to talk to you." He shoved the blaster back in its holster and turned.

Kathy followed dutifully, realizing he was just as disgusted at being their hound dog as she was at being summoned like some obedient pet.

Now, she really wished she had one of the Terran transpods.

* * *

"Half-breed!"

Theresa Appaloosa turned and smiled at the Equy trotting beside her, his bulk easily double hers. "Don't you wish you looked as good, horseface!" Her slim face and short snout were dainty compared to the cannon snout that he sported.

"You even smell like them," he said, throwing his mane disdainfully over his shoulder.

Cute, Theresa thought, amused by his haughtiness. "Stallion as big as you should be careful not to trip over yourself."

His ears focused forward, alerting her to his interest. Ever so subtly, he edged closer, the long, wide spaceport esplanade easily accommodating them and all the passers-by without need for crowding. "Little filly like you might find yourself with more stallion than you can take at one time."

For all his dislike of her Terran half, he seemed pretty attracted to her Equy half. "I guess I'll have to take that stallion more than once, won't I?"

He whinnied, bucking a little.

She could see he was trotting with a slightly wider stance. She looked along the concourse ahead, saw the gate where her flight to the Horsehead Nebula wouldn't arrive for another two hours, saw the lavatory just before it, and turned to grin at him. "What's your name, handsome?" And she sidled into him to guide him the direction she wanted to go.

He was as long and full as she'd hoped, and her being so small meant a much tighter fit, and she felt his mounting pleasure, hers mounting with his, and he might have had a firehose as her bellows squeezed him dry, dribbles down her legs and puddles around her hooves.

"You're under arrest!"

Hot waves of guilt and shame washed over her. Theresa had never felt so embarrassed, gathering her clothes around her as they led her away, her hindquarters sopping wet and quivering still.

As the van door shut behind her, the gravcart rising to take her off to jail, Theresa cursed the Terran male who'd wooed her mother with such passion in the days before their planet had succumbed to the unrelenting hordes of the Terran Emperor Chingis Khan some twenty-eight years before. She cursed the Terran male whose passion his child clearly shared, this her fourth time having been apprehended in flagrante dilecto, albeit never in so public a place. She cursed the Terran half that Equy males so desired, their throbbing members finding her hot spot ...

Theresa sighed, knowing she was doomed with the same passion as her father. Angry at herself, she wished she had one of the Terran transpods. With them, the Terrans had conquered the quadrant in six short years. As she swayed in the van with each of its turns, she thought dreamily how it must have been for her parents, one widowed in the hard-fought war, the other inflamed with the lust of the kill and the thrill of the victory.

The van pulled to a stop, and an old mare opened the doors. "We'll take her from here, Charlie."

Theresa straightened her clothes once again and followed the female into the building. "Where are you taking me?"

"The Imperials want to talk to you, but before they do, let's get you cleaned up."

Theresa followed, wondering what the Terrans wanted. They'll be like my father, she thought, having never met him, having seen just one Terran in her life, and that from a distance.

If only I had one of their transpods, Theresa thought, then I could just disappear.

Chapter 2

"Your father wanted you to have this."

The amulet instantly devoured Amber's attention, like a sprig of cat-nip. A gold ring of metal surrounded an almost-translucent, porcelain-like material, and in the center was what looked to be a crystal or some type of quartz. She turned it over, the same on both sides.

Forgotten were the constant looks from other Fellies, the jibes, the slights, the giggles, the smiles behind the paws, the knowing twitch of a whisker, the distant shout of "Half-breed!"

And sometimes not so distant.

"Quick, put it away before somebody sees," her mother hissed. Her mother a Calico, she wore brown and black patches down either side of a white spine, and sported two black ears above fine white cheeks. The two of them had been left alone for a moment in a deserted hallway at the police station.

Shortly after her arrival, the politburo fat-cat had entered the corridor outside the tank. Amber might not have noticed her but for the salutes she got from the uniforms. She'd extended a single claw in Amber's direction, and then soon after they'd taken her to an interrogation room. "You have a choice, Amber Calico," the fat-cat told her before leaving her by herself. "Face charges of assault, get convicted, serve your sentence, and be turned over to the Imperials, or …" The polit-bitch smiled, whiskers curling back from her nose. "Go with them now."

Amber realized in a few short minutes that the Felly Government really didn't have a choice. They'd been told to remand her unto Imperial custody, no ifs and or buts. To save face, they'd protested she was facing charges of assault. Only if she chose to go could they legitimately say they hadn't caved obsequiously to Imperial demands, as other worlds and races had so subserviently done—the Cannies being the most obvious example.

The Canny homeworld had capitulated not long after the Terrans had come hurtling out of their system on the inner Perseus Arm, for which the Cannies were universally maligned.

"Why?" Amber had asked.

The fat polit-bitch looked startled. "Why what?"

"Why do they want me? Why are they seeking my extradition?"

The eyes dropped to the floor, then looked to the side. She shook her head finally and frowned, whiskers drooping. "We don't know."

Now, standing in the corridor, the amulet tucked in her sash, her mother embracing her for what Amber was sure was the last time, she asked her mother the same question. "What do they want with me?"

"I don't know," her mother said flatly.

"You do know," Amber replied flatly, seeing the answer in her mother's eyes. Twenty-four years old and long since accepting of her mother's faults, she shrugged. "And either you can't tell me here and now, or you don't think I'm ready to hear it. I'll trust your judgment on that."

Her mother glanced down the hall. "I love you."

The politburo fat-cat looked their direction.

Can't tell me here, Amber decided. "I love you too." They embraced.

"Time to go," the fat-cat said, approaching, her ears low.

She kissed her mother on the cheek and followed the bureau-cat to the roof.

There shimmered a transpod.

The egg-shaped, smooth-shelled transpod looked semi-translucent. Some trick of the eye or illusion of the mind caused the objects behind it to appear briefly. It was difficult to look at, because its shimmer—the rapid flickering of the object and the brief appearance of everything behind it—caused her to think it wasn't really there.

"Just don't look closely at it," the fat-cat said. "It'll drive you crazy. They tell me these things don't really exist right here. They occupy some space-time fold of their own, which is how they get around so fast."

The fact that one had been dispatched to retrieve her bewildered Amber.

The side door opened as they approached. Inside was one seat.

"In you go."

The interior looked far more solid than the shimmering exterior. Amber didn't hesitate. She had no hope of a somewhat normal life on Felly. But how would her destination be any different, wherever she was going? Reviled by the Terrans for her half-Felly status or reviled by the Felly for her half-Terran status? What was the difference, really?

She climbed in, thought about buckling the restraints but decided not to, found the seat comfortable, as though designed for her frame.

The door closed, and through the translucent shell, streaks of light replaced the rooftop, and a shock hurled her against the ceiling.

* * *

"Your father wanted you to have this."

The amulet instantly drew Kathy's attention, pulling on her mind like a luscious bone to chew on. A gold ring of metal encircled a porcelain-like material that was almost translucent, and the center looked to be a crystal or some type of quartz. It looked the same from both sides.

Forgotten were the stares from other Cannies, the low growls, the subtle slights, the snickers, the giggles, the smiles behind the paws, the knowing twitch of a moistened nostril, the distant bark of "Half-breed!"

"Quick, put it away before somebody sees it," her mother growled.

Kathy tucked away the amulet.

The detective had escorted Kathy from the university library to a hover, which had whisked them to police headquarters. He'd shown her to a small, stuffy office in the basement, seeming rather proud of its Spartan look. "I'm in missing persons, not a position likely to garner more than a bone to a dog, you know?"

"I'm a 'missing persons'?"

"One agency's junk is another agency's treasure."

"Listen, you swayback mongrel—"

"Cool it, girl, I was giving you a compliment, if you'd keep your yap shut long enough to listen."

She'd opened her mouth to excoriate him, but something about the glint in his eye ... A subvocal growl rippled along her jowl. "Out with it, dick-face."

"You just don't know when to cork it, eh?" the detective said to Kathy. "No matter. Supposedly, those Terrans like that in a grrl. Here's the wag: An all-sectors bulletin goes out for a thirty-year-old, half-Canny, half-Terran female fitting your description. Reason? Get this: 'Possible offspring from conquest of Canis Major.' Nothing more. Me, I *am* missing persons, see the bulletins all the time. This one smells bad all around, so I go sniffing further. Us bloodhounds equipped for it, right? What do I get for my curiosity? I nearly get sent to the doghouse, threatened with demotion to patrol! Patrol! An old dog like me, learning new tricks? Forget about it! And for what? A little sniffing? Must've stuck my snout in the wrong crotch is all I can figure. Whoever's got their nose to the ground for you isn't to be taken lightly, so careful with that yap of yours, all right? Now, I've commed your dam cause she's gotta be worried ..."

And he'd let her meet with her mother privately. Kathy looked deeply into her mother's eyes. "Who was my father, really?"

Biting her lip, her mother looked down and away.

All along, Kathy had hated this one obscure fact about her parentage, that her mother wouldn't or couldn't tell her about her father or even talk about him—always the bitten tongue, the blinked-back tears, the quivering jowl, the averted gaze.

"Ma, look at me." Kathy wasn't about to let it happen again. "You have to tell me. You have to."

"They're a bit early, I'm afraid," the detective said, stepping between them and taking Kathy by the elbow.

"Keep you paws off me, snout-face. Goodbye, Ma. I guess I'll just have to trust you, as difficult as that is right now. I love you." And she hugged her mother for what she knew would be the last time.

Doggedly following the dick through the basement corridors, Kathy sighed, wondering what sort of persuasion had been used on her mother to prevent her from revealing information that Kathy had requested persistently since age four, when she'd learned that she was somehow different because her father had been Terran.

On one occasion, her mother had lost patience with Kathy's needling. "Anything! Ask me anything, anything at all! Except that! Anything except that!" And then she'd wept.

Kathy hadn't asked as frequently after that, but her curiosity had only doubled. She'd frequently found her way to the district archive, attached for hours to the neurimmerser, trying to match her own features with face after Terran face. After the Canny capitulation, hundreds of thousands of soldiers, diplomats, businessmen, and contractors had arrived in waves. The features of Canny and Terran being so disparate, computer modeling hadn't helped her find a match either, and after a few years, she had given up. But she still asked the question periodically, despite the suffering she caused her mother by asking it.

Following the detective through the building basement, Kathy saw they approached a little-used corner, what might have once been a night guard's quarters. Even from beyond the door, she saw the weird light.

In the corner room, barely large enough for a bed and a desk, was an egg-shaped, smooth-shelled transpod. It looked semi-translucent, objects behind it flickering briefly into view, making it difficult to look at. I wonder if it's really there, Kathy thought.

"I'm told it doesn't really exist—not right here anyway. Sits in some space-time fold all its own, they say."

"They sent one for me?" Kathy was alarmed.

The side opened as she stepped near, looking far more solid on the inside than out. Inside was a single seat.

"In you go."

Kathy didn't hesitate. Clutching the amulet tightly, she climbed in, glad to be shut of the constant Canny disapproval for her half-Terran parentage, without hope for a normal life among her mother's people.

But what about there? she wondered. Could she expect anything different from the Terrans? Would they revile her just the same for her half-Canny genes?

Resigned, she thought, What's the difference, really?

The seat was comfortable, as though designed for her frame, Kathy larger than most Terrans but smaller than most Cannies.

She buckled the restraints, and the door closed. Through the translucent shell, streaks of light replaced the basement, the shock hurling her against the restraints.

* * *

"Your father wanted you to have this."

"Why couldn't he have wanted me to have a normal life?" Theresa snapped.

The blow turned her head, and tears leaped into her eyes. Her mother had never struck her before! Theresa couldn't believe it!

"He gave you life and a whole lot more than that, if you'd only open your eyes to see it, if you'd only open your hands to take it."

Theresa looked down at what her mother proferred.

The amulet instantly secured all of Theresa's attention, glinting even in the dim light of the loading dock, a gold ring of metal surrounding a translucent disk of porcelain, and in the center a chunk of crystal or quartz. She turned it over, saw it looked the same from both sides.

Forgotten were the resentments she'd harbored against her mother for falling in love with a Terran, the bitterness of growing up fatherless, the long nights imagining all the things she'd do with the father she'd always wanted, the public events where all her peers had their dams and sires watching over them proudly, while all her mother could do was avert her face in shame that no sire stood beside them.

"Put it away before somebody sees it," her mother nickered.

Theresa tucked it away in a pocket and kept her hand over it as though afraid its brilliance would shine through the fabric of her formalls.

She'd been escorted by the foreign office attaché to a locker room deep underneath the spaceport, where she'd bathed and dressed. For all its form-fitting seams, sleeves, and snaps, the formal was ill-fitting at best, her substantially smaller hybrid form difficult to clothe in standard Equy dress. "Your mother wants to see you—but it has to be brief. They'll be here soon."

The attaché had taken her to a nondescript door leading into a loading dock, where her mother had been waiting.

Amulet in pocket, Theresa looked up at her mother, who stood two hands taller than she—and always would. At twenty-eight, Theresa was full grown. "Petite" she'd always been called, which she'd hated. Looking up at her dam, she saw the years of suffering suddenly manifest in her face, the guilt of a mother powerless to do better for a child.

"What was Father like?"

The guilt and suffering fled her mother's face, replaced with deep adoration. "He was a wonderful man."

It was all Theresa needed. It was all she'd ever needed, just to know he had treated her mother well.

"And you're a wonderful girl." Her mother wrapped her in her arms.

"They're here," the attaché said, peeking out onto the loading dock. She practically tore Theresa from her mother's embrace.

"I love you, Ma," she said, catching a last glimpse of her mother's tear-filled eyes before the door closed between them.

"Sorry about the abrupt departure. We've got a situation."

Theresa heard the panic in the voice as she followed the filly through corridors and up stairwells.

"They've changed their minds. Instead of coming here, they've sent a transpod for you. Never been in one, probably, right? Me, either. Seen one or two, difficult to look at. I'm not sure why the change in plans. I suspect things are happening at the seat of power. Big things. Never seen 'em send a transpod for one of ours. Whoever wants you on Earth has real pull. This way."

The attaché led Theresa into a large room nearly devoid of furniture. In the center sat a smooth-shelled egg, four hands taller than her. The egg looked semi-transparent, objects behind it flickering briefly into view.

Theresa squinted at it, blinking, not really sure what she was looking at.

"They tell me it doesn't really exist, right here, anyway. Occupies some time-space fold somewhere."

Theresa found it disconcerting that one had been sent for her.

The side opened, revealing an interior that looked far more substantial than the ethereal shell.

"In you go."

The seat was comfortable, as if built for her frame. Odd, she thought, as though they knew my dimensions. She buckled the restraints and slipped a hand into her pocket to touch the amulet, wishing her mother well.

Not her fault I was born such a freak, Theresa thought, glad to be shut of the Equy in general. Most Equies towered over her and weighed half again as much. The worst had been the constant doting, the feeble attempts by uncomfortable Equies to fawn over her childlike countenance, even by some younger than she was. I won't miss any of it, Theresa told herself.

What will it be like among Terrans? she wondered. Could she expect anything different? She certainly wouldn't be the smallest among them. Would they revile her for her half-Equy genes, welcome her as a novelty, laugh at her pronounced barrel face, so different from those flat-faced Terrans?

Theresa sighed, apprehensive.

The door closed, and through the translucent shell, streaks of light replaced the room, the shock throwing her against the restraints.

Chapter 3

Amber Calico groaned on the floor of the transpod, pulsating pain bringing her out of unconsciousness. What happened? she wondered, waiting to see whether she'd be shaken apart further.

For ten minutes following her departure, the transpod had wobbled violently, throwing her from one side to the other. Then something had hit her head and she'd lost consciousness.

Through the transparent shell, the surface of a cratered moon was visible. The gravity corresponded; she could have lifted herself with one finger.

She searched her aching head with a paw to see if she were bleeding and tested her limbs to see if any were broken. Her vestigial tail hurt badly from her full weight coming down on it, but that appeared to be the worst injury. Mostly bruises and scrapes, other than losing consciousness.

I wished I'd strapped myself in, Amber thought. She'd not had time enough to get herself secured, the pod shaking too violently.

Dragging herself into the chair, she looked over the instruments. Her position was three-fourths the way up the Perseus Arm, on the other side of Earth from the Cat's Eye Nebula, her homeworld now a long way away. Wherever the transpod was supposed to have taken her, Amber knew she hadn't arrived.

What sort of forsaken hole did I land on? she wondered.

The pod rested in the bottom of a crater, and she couldn't see beyond its lip. A cloud-shrouded planet hung in the sky, blotting out any stars she might have seen.

A sensor on the panel warned her that the moon had no atmosphere, a fact plainly obvious from the rocky terrain. Where do I get an airshell? she wondered. I'll bet these transpods come equipped with them.

A brief search revealed a cubby under the seat.

She strapped the airshell around her waist, having to tighten it to its smallest size. Probably not expecting that I'd need it, she thought. The airshell crinkled around her as she opened the transpod door. The cold nipped at her fingers, toes, and ears before the airshell compensated. Her ears plastered to her head in dismay, Amber stepped onto the dirt.

Closing the transpod door, she wondered what to do with it. On the Felly homeworld, transpods were forbidden, all the subjugated worlds of the Terran Empire prohibited from having or using them.

I can't just leave it here, she thought, knowing someone was likely to see it, detect it, or perhaps even retrace her strange journey to find it. To find her.

Suspecting something had gone awry, Amber didn't want to be found. Unable to do anything with the transpod, she left it there. Fingering the amulet in her pocket, she climbed toward the crater rim.

The bright lights of the small city nearly blinded her.

She ducked back below the rim, wondering if anyone had seen her. She peeked—too far away.

She glanced again at the planet hovering in the sky and realized she was looking at its nightside, and her eyes, adapted for even the darkest night, had adjusted.

"Beep."

What was that? she wondered, looking around briefly.

Her irises vertical slits, she gazed upon the moon city, easily a klik away, searching for signs of activity. It wasn't as large as she'd initially thought, just brightly lit. Five hundred occupants, she estimated.

She climbed onto the crater lip and looked back.

The transpod was gone!

As her brain stumbled over the fact, her eyes searched the crater.

Nothing.

Then she realized: The transpod had sat at the exact center.

"Beep."

What was that? she wondered, looking around briefly.

Further, she also saw that the crater was perfect, unmarred by meteor strikes or tire tracks, unmarked by footprints except her own, perfectly undisturbed by anything except her own activity.

The impact of the transpod had made the crater!

Lucky I'm not dead, Amber realized, the volume of displacement indicating a high-velocity impact.

Really high-velocity.

"Freeze!" said a deep male voice.

Shocked to hear a voice, Amber almost didn't.

"Turn around slowly!" the voice was coming from her airshell!

Made sense that it had a built in optimitter. Without air, no speech. Having never been off-world, Amber realized just how much she didn't know. And how will the light gravity affect my balance and my ability to fight? she wondered.

She turned slowly.

Twelve barrels were pointed at her.

"Told you it was Felly," said a soft contralto voice. The woman standing next to the man in the lead was a big Canny, her long floppy ears hanging nearly to her shoulders, her hide a patchwork of brown and white.

The man was Terran, oily black curls falling nearly to his waist, a gaudy silk vest and tasseled silk pants looking almost silly on the sere moon surface. "What's your name?" Around his neck was a silver locket on a chain.

"Amber. Amber Ripclaw." Her fighting name, in case they were searching for her under her real name.

"Where'd your ship go?" the Canny female asked, peering into the crater. "Quite the crash. Set off the seismic monitors back at the bar. Thought we'd come out in case the meteor left behind some valuable metal. But it's just you—without a trace of the ship you arrived in."

Amber wished she knew. "I was knocked out by the impact. When I came to ..." She shrugged.

The Canny woman stepped up to her, so close that their airshells crackled. "Liar." And she swung.

Amber ducked, and with two swift punches and a kick, she laid out the Canny on her back.

The blasters hadn't wavered.

The man was roaring with laughter, his barrel unwavering. "Smitty, carry Miss Minoa back to the bar. And you, Miss Amber Felly with the fake last name, you'll come with me."

* * *

Kathy Mongrel tried to make her eyes focus and her stomach behave, still dizzy from the wild spinning and multiple shocks across the last ten minutes. She waited a moment to see if more were coming.

Glad I had the restraints on, she thought, I might have broken some bones if I hadn't.

A blast of green slime leaped from her mouth and splashed the dash, most of it dropping right into her lap, the gravity heavy. Kathy heaved again but dryly.

And again.

Laying back in the chair, she tried to focus on the terrain visible through the transparent shell. Her eyes wouldn't focus. A small voice in the back of her head said that transpod travel probably wasn't supposed to be like that.

The smell of her own vomit and the battering and spinning across the last ten minutes were too much, and she began to weep.

A slimed light on the dash alerted her that the atmosphere beyond the shell was seventy percent ammonia.

I'll need an airshell, Kathy thought, despairing again and afraid the transpod would throw her into another wild cyclone. There must be an airshell in here, she thought. Bending down to inspect the seat she sat on caused her to heave again, but she found the cubby underneath.

The belt was on its last notch. I guess they weren't expecting me to need this. She opened the door and stumbled out, the airshell sparkling as it repelled the noxious ammonia wind.

What's that howling? she wondered, thinking it was a wounded dog. Then she realized it was the wind singing through rock crevices.

The transpod lay at the bottom of a gully whose sides of jagged rock were bare of foliage.

Not much likely to grow in an atmosphere like this, she thought. She looked up the gully side, felt how difficult it was just to stand in the heavy gravity, and knew she'd hate every moment of the climb. Having spent most of the last eight years in college, she wasn't in very good shape.

Pushing herself up the slope, Kathy quickly grew winded, her airshell fan screaming, struggling to replace the air around her.

She rested halfway to the lip, her paws and nose sweating, her forehead hot, her tongue hanging to one side from her mouth.

"Beep, Beep."

What was that? she wondered, looking around.

The transpod was gone.

Kathy looked around to see who'd taken it.

No one.

Wrapped in her airshell, the ammonia winds howling around her, she wouldn't have likely heard them anyway. Where did it go?

Shaking her head, she climbed to the lip.

Halfway down the far slope was a domed structure, beyond it a yawning chasm so wide that the raveling mists gave her just glimpses of the other side.

After catching her breath, she climbed down toward the domed structure, the lighted windows indicating occupancy, the upper floor obscured by curtains, the lower looking like dining and kitchen areas.

I sure could eat something right now.

Cycling herself through the airlock, Kathy felt the airshell collapse from around her, the scents of cinnamon and lavender bringing her peace.

"Beep, beep."

She spun to see where the noise was coming from. Her pocket! She pulled out the amulet. The crystal glowed with a dull orange light. Kathy put her fingertip on the crystal, and her surroundings shimmered as though ethereal. She took her finger off immediately.

"It's you!"

Kathy leaped backward and slammed into the door.

A bearded Terran stood at the base of the stairs. "You've come and not a moment too soon. Quickly, this way!" He turned and trotted up the stairs, said down the stairwell, "Now, young lady!"

Her obedience instinct responded before she could intervene, and she found herself at the top of the stairs.

"Look!"

On a holo screen was a wall-size bust shot of the Terran Emperor Chingis Khan, who had laid waste to his enemies and conquered three-fourths of the Perseus Arm in ten short years, then had ruled those domains with an iron fist for the next twenty.

Dead at age sixty, the subtext said.

On a chain at the base of his throat was a porcelain disc rimmed with gold, a crystal mounted in the center.

Kathy felt faint.

"I see you're beginning to understand," the old Terran said. "Come with me. We have to leave before they get here. And put that amulet away before somebody sees it!" He leaped down the stairs, far more spry than she thought he should be at his age, Kathy scrambling to follow.

They dropped to a third level, where an airship was coming to life. Its doors already open, they leaped inside, and the airship rocketed from underneath the house, blowing through the door before it was fully open.

Behind them, the home dome disintegrated in a fireball.

* * *

Her insides shaken to a pulp, Theresa Appaloosa waited anxiously to see if the shaking would begin again. For the last ten minutes, the transpod had gyrated wildly in all directions, and beyond the transparent shell, kaleidoscopic colors had cavorted.

After a minute of inactivity, she dared to peek.

The transpod sat on a shelf—a large shelf. By its appearances a continental shelf. Thousands of feet below, an ocean roiled bitterly, wind-whipped whitecaps ripped into raveling spray. On the shelf where the transpod sat, coarse grasses waved under a battery of gusts, looking as though they clung precariously to the soil itself.

It looks so uninviting, Theresa thought.

A green light on the transpod dash indicated an oxygen atmosphere.

A small bonus, she thought, wondering what she'd have done if the transpod had landed on an asteroid.

I don't think the trip was supposed to be like that, she thought idly, unbuckling herself and opening the transpod door.

The sea-freshened atmosphere rushed in, bringing the smell of thick grass. The Equy race derived from plains-grazers, Theresa began to drool, her powerful jaw muscles clenching as though already chewing.

The sod underneath her hooves felt good, her instinct to drop to all fours and gallop away across the headland.

She turned to look at the transpod. What do I do with it? she wondered, the egg-shaped device flickering intermittently. No place to hide it, and I don't want anyone to find it.

Theresa peered over the cliff.

Nearly a straight drop.

Well, she thought, if the trip here didn't damage the pod, neither will a short drop.

She dropped to all fours, put her backside to the pod, and leaned forward to plant a hind kick. The transpod arced gracefully out over the water and plummeted.

Then disappeared.

Theresa blinked.

No splash, no wave, just roiling sea. Swearing she didn't see it strike water, she turned to look inland.

Whoever had sent her on that wild journey in the transpod was likely to come looking for her soon. She put her head down and set off at a gallop, intending to be elsewhere.

The terrain sloped gently upward, grasses thickening and stalks growing taller. Soon the way was obscured, the grasses so tall that Theresa had to follow what appeared to be a game trail. The path bifurcated and she chose one at random, not stopping to consider. Down into a ravine it took her, and she realized that the opposite slope was honeycombed with tunnels.

She slowed, realizing the formation was unnatural.

The deep ravine ahead was lined with people, funny-looking, flop-eared people, a ridge of fur upon each head.

Halting, she stood on her hind legs, her breathing rough, a slight lather on her flank.

They were all peering at her from the safety of their burrows.

Terran? she wondered, able only to see their upper torso, their heads hairy, some of their faces too.

"Hello," Theresa said.

Half of them disappeared at the sound, and a flurry of rapid chatter chided her from under the hillside.

A tall being in a long tunic with a belt approached. The hair was long and red, the face hairless, the eyes green and sharp. Words issued from the mouth, followed by chatter from the belt, neither of which Theresa understood.

"I'm Equy, from Epsilon Eridani near the Horsehead Nebula. My name is Theresa."

The person spoke again, and the box squawked, "Equy? Why didn't you say so? You don't look Equy. What do you want?"

Tell them the truth? she wondered, sensing their distrust. If I were a cave dweller, I wouldn't trust me either. "I'm half-Equy, half-Terran. My transpod malfunctioned and dumped me here. I'm afraid I'm being chased. Can you help me, please?"

"Why should I help you, half-breed?" The box squawking at the waist was somewhat disconcerting. "Your half-brethren enslaved my people and cause us to live like this, in burrows underground. They rain fire upon us when they find us, or snatch us up in nets to be put to work in their dirty factories. Why should I help your Terran half, half-breed?"

The taunts of childhood stung anew. Theresa blinked back tears. "Because the Equy struggle to throw off the yoke of the Terran oppressor just like you! My dam tells me we were a happy people before the conquest, and now all we do is natter and backbite amongst ourselves. Were you so suspicious before the Terrans came? Would you turn out a wanderer seeking food and shelter simply because they were not of your herd?"

The face softened. "We were not and we would not. I'm Leila. Come on, then, and see the latest news of our mutual oppressor."

Sighing, Theresa followed. The burrow entrance was a tight fit for her frame, but once inside, the tunnels opened enough that she could trot on all fours. She followed Leila deep into the hillside, the darkened tunnels occasionally lit by a slim pipe to the surface. The air would quickly stale without them, she realized.

The great room opened before her like a theater, along one wall a viewscreen, and wide steps marching up toward the back. As her eyes adjusted, Theresa realized from the smell and the number that this was where they lived, all clustered in one big den, some forty-five of them, she estimated.

Having come in from the side, Theresa saw that nearly all of them were paying her no mind, their attention fixed to the screen.

On it, a Terran bust looked them over, and at the bottom in Terran were the words, "Emperor Chingis Khan, dead at age sixty." Around his neck was a chain, and on it at the base of his throat was a porcelain disk with a gold rim and a crystal mounted in the center.

Theresa gasped, her hand going to the amulet in her pocket. It felt warm to the touch. That's what was beeping! she thought, not daring to take it out now, in front of all these strangers.

"These events foretell a change, friend Theresa. We thought his enslavement of us was terrible, but now we face an heir who might be more terrible still, would that we knew. Tis true they enslave and oppress us, work us in their factories sunrise to set. Yes, but they feed us, clothe us, house us. Before they came, we had not much more than you see. Our higher arts were a tale around a hearth, a traveling bard to sing us a song. We grazed innocently upon our abundant grasses, the stewards of our modest domains. Space travel? Burrow to burrow was all our imaginations might conceive. Science? Devoted to cultivating richer, more succulent grasses. We knew not predator nor competitor, had no need to look beyond the reach of the paws we hold at arm's length.

"Until they came." Leila turned to the screen. "We have no means to fight these scurrilous creatures, our peaceful natures without the warring instinct. We cower like scared rabbits—a Terran phrase by the way—in our burrows and dens, our only wish to have the liberties we once enjoyed returned to us." Leila turned to Theresa. "What of you, traveler?"

She shook her head. "I was summoned to Earth by means of a transpod, perhaps because my father was Terran, but something went awry and I landed here."

"Transpod? You still have it?"

Theresa shook her head. "I was afraid I might be traced, so I kicked it into the ocean. I didn't know how to operate it. I saw no controls. I guess I'm stuck on this planet until I find a way … home."

Leila looked at the floor. "I sense it's a home that isn't a home. I called you a name you didn't deserve. I saw the tears. My apologies. That was hurtful to you."

Theresa shook her head. "An old hurt, borne many years, and not inflicted by you. But thank you for the apology." She looked of the viewscreen. "What now? What will become of the Empire that this monster inflicted upon the rest of us?"

Leila shrugged, two furry paws spreading open. "They search for an heir, a Terran heir, of course. There is a boy but yet a babe. His is a fate I wouldn't wish on anyone, for if Terrans are as I've seen them do, they will fight over him throughout his infancy and seek to mold him to their designs. Many factions will seek to claim his regency and rule in his stead until he is of age to do so himself."

Leila turned to look at Theresa. "It will be a tumultuous time."

Chapter 4

"What do you want from me?" Amber growled, hair bristling along her spine. She stood across the room from the Terran in the gaudy outfit, two of his guards on either side of him, their weapons trained on her.

Nearby, the Canny female was just coming to, her big floppy frame draped across an armchair.

"With fighting skills like that," the Terran gestured at the drowsy Canny, "what do you think I want?"

Amber sighed, telling herself she was lucky they hadn't cut her apart.

"She just got lucky," the Canny named Minoa mumbled, a paw to her jowl.

"Come here, Minny," the ring-haired Terran said, crooking a finger at her.

"I know what you're thinking, Boss, and I promise I'll be good. I recognized a good fighter just as you do, and I won't let personal animosity get in the way of a professional relationship." Minny got to her feet and stretched. "You got me a fair and square, Miss Felly, and I can respect that. Besides, we got bigger cats to skin, right, Boss?"

"Right, Minny. Look at this, Miss Felly," and Boss gestured at the side wall opposite the big dog Minny.

"My name's Calico, Amber Calico."

"All right, Calico," Boss said. "Take a look."

A bust appeared, captioned, "Emperor Chingis Khan, dead at age sixty." Around his neck was a chain, and at the base of his throat was a porcelain disk with a gold rim and a crystal at the center.

What the tenth life is going on? Amber wondered, reaching into her pocket. She left her hand there, carefully keeping her face blank. "So the Emperor's dead. So what? Not my affair. He can rot in that Terran afterlife they're always babbling about."

"Ahh, but it *is* our affair," Boss said, a grin on his face. "We're pirates, and chaos in the Empire means easier pickings for us. Of course, we need people to go and take it. You've got a mean left cross. Why not put it to work for us?"

Amber glanced from Boss to Minoa. "I'd rather be on my way. I need to get to Earth."

Minoa snorted. "Earth? It'll be so overrun with ne'er-do-wells and schemers and sycophants that they'll close up the planet like a turtle and all you'll do is bounce off the shell. Why do you want to go there, anyway?"

Amber shrugged and glanced at the still. "I was being summoned by..." And she realized she didn't know who or why.

"You? A Felly?" Boss peered at her. "Half-Felly? I don't think you want to go there. Minny, why don't you show her around, get her something to eat, see if that'll convince her it's not so urgent to get to Earth? Think about it for a day or two, Amber. Earth will be there while you make up your mind."

Minoa led her from the room, introducing Amber to her fellow pirates, a motley mixture of races who shared an oppressor: Ursy, Porcy, Taury, Bouy, Murry—all the conquered civilizations.

Wrapped in airshells, they walked toward a brightly-lit building, multiple people visible through the windows. "Canteen" said the sign above the door. Of the hundred or so buildings visible, only that and "Hangar" were labeled. Just inside the hanger doors, the prow of a large ship was visible.

At the canteen door, a loud cheer went up at their entrance, Amber dismayed at the volume. When it didn't subside, she realized no one had given them the slightest bit of attention, that the besotted crowd was simply loud.

Minoa guided her through the chow line, the terrified kitchen crew cowering at the Canny's bulk, their tentacles quivering. "Measly roaches," Minoa muttered, heading toward a table in front of the largest vidscreen Amber had ever seen, on it a Terran yapping silently. Amber looked at her plate of food, not sure she wanted to eat something from a cockroach-infested kitchen.

The table was packed. Minoa gave a push and a shove, and suddenly two places were clear.

Amber sat down, trying to ignore the goo she set in her tray in. "What are they saying?"

Minoa shrugged and leaned across the table, slapped a drunk and out popped his earpiece.

Amber examined it, wiped if the best she could, then perched it near her ear.

"... Wrosnaya brinskinisha svobradaski ..."

She looked for a place on her airshell belt to plug it into. There.

"... death of the Emperor Khan is being greeted all along the Perseus Arm with an outpouring of sorrow—" The vid switched to a weeping crowd of Terrans—"and expressions of condolence for the sole heir, the one-year-old Kublai Khan—" switched to an infant headshot, the face twisted with displeasure—"whose installment as Emperor is being prepared as we speak."

"You really don't believe any of that drivel, do you?" Minoa asked.

Amber shook her head, eating doggedly and trying not to look too closely at what she was eating. "I'll wager the kid never sees his second birthday."

"I'll bet you're right. Look, Amber, ain't nothing there for you." Minoa waved at the screen. "Those Terrans, all they think about is money."

"Boss any different?"

"Not really, except that he takes care of us all. What I'm saying is, you, me, and Boss, and every little critter crawling the ground like we are, we don't mean a thing to the Emperor and his cronies. There's twenty people along the Perseus Arm who have any real power or wealth. Most are Terrans, with one or two of us in there. All the rest of us, just slaves to their designs. Here on the edge, we make our own way. Not the best food, or the best accommodations—"

The bare plastic benches attest to that! Amber thought.

"—but it's ours. We raid what we want, when we want, and how we want, and having to fight off the occasional Imperial battlecruiser or patrol is a minor price to pay for that freedom."

Amber felt Minoa's eyes upon her as she continued to eat, the food bland but filling even so.

Minoa picked up her glass and drained the greenish bubbly fluid.

Amber sniffed hers, smelled the intoxicant. "Any water?"

Minoa blew a spray, erupting in laughter, their tablemates across from them protesting the shower. "That's royal, Amber! I like that." Minoa pounded her on the back, laughing uncontrollably.

Amber set down her glass before it spilled, the pounding nearly causing her to wretch. And they want me to stay? she wondered, smiling at Minoa but frowning inside.

The vid had switched back to a montage of the deceased Emperor at various ages and various guises. Amber saw in nearly all the vids and stills that he wore the porcelain disk ringed with gold, the crystal at the center glinting with reflected light.

After the meal, Minoa led her to an unsightly abode beside headquarters. "You can room with me until we find you a bunk."

The divan was less than divine, covered with Canny hair. And probably infested with fleas, Amber thought. Laying awake in the dark, she stared at the ceiling, the soft snore from the next room interrupted occasionally by a low growl or soft bark, the Canny having gone instantly to sleep.

Stay or go? Amber kept wondering, a yawn overtaking her. Then she reprimanded herself. You know full well this isn't what you wanted, and the only thing keeping you here is the lack of a way to get off this rock!

She sat up and took the amulet out of her pocket.

The crystal in the center glowed with a dim blue light.

The disk, she saw, fit nicely within the circle of her thumb and forefinger.

The moment she closed them around the rim, the room shimmered.

Alarmed, she dropped it into her other hand, the shimmer disappearing. Almost as though I was back in the transpod, she thought, shaking her head and wondering if she were simply so tired that she'd hallucinated.

Amber lay back down and closed her eyes, but sleep would not come. The soft snore from the next room seemed to taunt her.

Finally, she rose, donned her airshell, and slipped out the door, quiet as a cat. The "streets" were deserted. The buildings placed haphazardly, the layout was so random that the spaces between buildings couldn't rightly be called streets. The nose poking out the hangar doors was visible in the ethereal glow cast by the cloud-shrouded planet hovering above the moon.

There was enough light inside the hanger to see the odd collection of spacecraft assembled inside. Yachts, fighters, cruisers, tankers, freighters, scows, and patrols, every one of them festooned with weapons mounted on every available surface.

Amber realized how large the place was, and just how successful an operation the pirates ran. The number and variety of ships far exceeded the number of pirates to operate them.

As her eyes adjusted to the darkness inside the hangar, Amber realized that not all the ships were functional, parts strewn beside eviscerated hulks. Probably just can't get parts, she thought.

Looking among the ships closest to the doors, Amber picked out a fighter vehicle, the Imperial insignias burned off the sides, the fuselage bristling with blasters. Climbing in, she wished she knew how to fly one. The seat was comfortable and she yawned.

This is as good a place as any, she thought, taking out the amulet again to look at it in the dim light spilling through the hangar doors.

I wish I could get that transpod back, she thought, wanting to flee this desolate moon and its ragtag bag of pirates.

She pulled the restraints around her, thinking I'll just sleep here.

The buckle snicked into place, and the patrol dashboard came to life.

A shadow crossed the hangar doors.

Across the com came a panicked voice, "Imperial raid!"

* * *

"What was that all about?" Kathy yelped, looking at him.

"Pardon me a moment," the Terran replied, eyes on the flight path.

The ship rolled to port, throwing Kathy against the restraints, and a rock spire protruding from the canyon wall to starboard exploded, showering them with debris.

The ship rolled to starboard and dropped, the canyon wall just feet away. Then the Terran jerked backward on the controls, the engine screaming in protest. Open sky filled the forward viewport.

Kathy caught a glimpse of their pursuers, an Imperial fighter bristling with guns, the insignia prominent on the fuselage.

"Take out that little bauble of yours!" the Terran said, yanking the stick to starboard; a rocket passed them to port, the light of its propulsion hot on Kathy's nose.

The porcelain disc between two fingers, she stared at him, wide-eyed.

"Aren't you going to use it?" He pinched his thumb to forefinger, making a circle.

The canyon-side coming at them, she screamed and imitated him, the gold rim fitting neatly within the circle.

The rock wall shimmered, and their ship plunged through it like a fish through water. They burst into the next canyon, and the Terran took them deep, slowing the ship and landing under an overhang. He leaped from the vehicle and draped a rock-colored fabric over it; Kathy could just see the opposite wall some fifty meters away, her airshell crackling at the ammonia.

The Terran climbed back in. "Now we wait, but keep your little toy handy."

Kathy heard the calm in his voice but smelt his fear. Her own fear prickled along her spine. "What just happened? And what is it?" She stared at the amulet, not quite believing what had just happened.

His gaze flicked both ways along the canyon, the bottom so close that the roar of water was audible. "Time for that later, the fact that you have it—remarkable."

"Why?" Kathy asked, a question she'd never stopped asking throughout her life. And to the answers she'd received, she asked another, "Why?" She'd driven her mother to distraction with her pestering why's. "Some cult symbol?"

"A cult that can pray itself through solid rock?" He chuckled. "Try again."

In other words, think for yourself, he's saying, she thought. She didn't know who he was or what his biases were or which side he was on, if any. "How did you know what it does?" The amulet around the Emperor's neck came to mind. "When did you meet the Emperor?"

He chuckled again. "Where did you get it?"

"How long since you left the Emperor's service? What were you, a general, an attaché, a personal guard? Were you with him in the early years, when he conquered the Perseus Arm?"

Again, he chuckled but this time shook his head. "At an impasse, it seems." He took one last look either way along the canyon. "I think we're in the clear." He reached for the door as though to get out.

"Not so fast, all right? At least tell me your name."

"Before you've told me yours?" He snorted. "We may not have much time ... We'd better go before reinforcements arrive." He stepped out the door to reel in the camouflage netting, stowed it and got back in.

Kathy examined the disc between thumb and forefinger as he readied the ship for launch. "Your father wanted you to have this," her mother had told her. Looking at the pilot and her happenstance rescuer, she wondered if he'd fought alongside the Emperor and if he might have known her father.

"I'm Mengu Larine, former Lieutenant Colonel, Commander, Fifth Division of his majesty's Imperial Navy. I led the assault on your homeworld, Canis Majoris III."

The acceleration pushed her into her seat, the canyon walls flickering past them. He subjugated my people, Kathy thought, wondering why she felt no bitterness. "Pity we didn't put up more of a fight." The Canny had capitulated quickly to the Terran onslaught.

"You'd have been formidable," he replied, guiding the ship just feet above the roiling river surface.

"I'm Kathy Mongrel, by the way." Something about what he'd said bothered her. "You led the assault?"

He nodded, slowing the ship to navigate a treacherously narrow part of the canyon.

"Then I'm not here by chance," Kathy said, "Am I?"

* * *

Theresa woke and looked around, disoriented for a moment.

Then she remembered she'd stumbled upon a den of creatures with floppy ears and big teeth. Oppressed creatures, kept enslaved by their Terran conquerors. The horrific tales Leila had told her of the great machinery houses where most her brethren worked without respite three-fourths of each and every day …

The soft snores around her indicated they all slept.

She rose without disturbing the soft furry creatures who'd snuggled up to her. In the dim light, she picked her way toward the tunnel where she'd entered, wondering how she would find her way out, but guessing she'd find her way.

They'd fed her their succulent grasses and had entertained her with songs and tales, then they'd all bedded down together, the parents admonishing the children to quiet themselves, and they'd slept.

Now, emerging onto a hillside the next morning, Theresa reflected how welcomed she'd felt, how at home. She felt the temptation to stay, for despite being different from them all, she had felt none of the difference, so unlike the twenty-eight lonely years she'd spent on Equy Prime, everywhere she went someone reminding her of her difference, her half-breed status.

She stood on the hilltop, the eastern sky beginning to brighten, and wondered where to go from here.

"South."

Theresa whirled.

Beside her stood Leila.

"South lives a Terran who gives us no grief. Neither does she give succor, but only because our overlords would punish her for it. Her name is Chabi, and she may know something of your plight."

"Chabi. Such strange names, these Terrans. Thank you, Leila, for your hospitality. Their oppression will one day lift. Be sure of that."

"I work toward it with my every breath," Leila said. The two embraced and Theresa turned.

Galloping south on all fours, perhaps a klik from the coast, she'd put many kloms behind her before the sun rose.

A quarter way into the sky, the sun baked the thick grass, much of it wilting under the heat, but out to sea, to her right, a thick black cloud was building. Winds soon kicked up, and the clouds moved inland, blotting out the sun. Thick shimmers of mist obscured the distance, and her sweat turned to condensation, the mist turned to rain, and the wind turned to gale.

I could easily stumble past my destination, Theresa thought, her visibility cut to perhaps twenty meters. I could mistake that fence post for a stick, or that hedge for a bush.

The steepled roof beyond the hedge emerged. Grateful she'd found something, Theresa stopped beside the tall hedge.

"Stay on all fours. You're being followed."

Theresa was dumfounded, so startled that she obeyed.

A woman draped in a poncho stepped from behind the hedge, barely five feet. "Appaloo, you've returned!" She took hold of Theresa's mane and leaped astride her.

It took all her will not to buck the strange creature off her back, repulsed by the feel of something astride her.

"Wondered where you'd run off to, girl! There's a fine horse if I've ever seen one."

Floodlights flared and illuminated them in the rain, the source hovering five meters off the ground some twenty meters away. The hum of an antigrav unit became audible.

The woman threw her arm up to shield her eyes. "Turn that off, blast you!"

Theresa whinnied in complaint, throwing her head to one side, trying to turn away from the blinding light.

The hover dimmed its lights somewhat and dropped. "I'm patrol officer Stewart," said a man stepping out of the vehicle. "A transpod was spotted landing forty-five kloms north of here. Seen anyone?"

"No, Officer, can't say I have, been out looking for my steed, only to find she'd returned on her own. Sorry I can't help you."

"See anything, give us a call, all right?"

"Certainly, Officer." She waved and patted the side of Theresa's neck. "Be happy to do so."

The hover rose and continued heading south.

"Just walk around the house," the woman told her. "Sorry about this. My name is Chabi, Chabi Schahahaday."

Fuming, Theresa wanted to buck the Terran off and gallop away through the rain. The small woman's butt dug into her back, and the heels dug into her ribs. "Ouch! Are they gone yet? I can't believe I'm letting you do this!" Halfway around the house, the hover nowhere to be seen, Theresa stopped in her tracks. "Off! Filthy Terran. Now I'll never get clean!" She snorted in disgust while the Terran dismounted.

"Sorry about that. Best disguise I could come up with at the time. What's your name?"

"Theresa, Theresa Appaloosa." She snorted her disgust and stood to her full height, easily half a meter taller than the short Terran. She looked her over.

Under the rain-slicked poncho, Chabi wore what looked like a standard-issue formall except for the boots. The thick-soled high-top boots extended far up under the poncho.

Probably reach all the way to her armpits, Theresa thought.

"Nice to meet you," Chabi said, extending a hand.

Theresa extended her mud-covered hand and shook. "Leila sent me here, said you might be able to help."

"If helping mean avoiding those patrols, I guess I've already done that. Come in for a spell, and let's not stand here yakkin', in case they come back."

The abode was simple, a peaked ceiling above a two-room house, rugs across a wooden floor, a microfission heat source embedded in a rock hearth, pipes lining the walls to take the heated water to a small kitchenette and even smaller bathing area.

"Welcome, and have a seat. A cup of hot tea for your cold, wet bones?"

Theresa nodded glumly, remorseful at her earlier outburst.

"A quick tongue and a short memory make great companions." She stepped to the stove and began to gather cup and kettle. "That way, I don't rightly remember what I just blathered on about. So it was you the patrol was looking for. Leila wouldn't have sent you this way if you weren't. What can I help you with?"

Theresa snorted. "Can't say I know, except that my transpod malfunctioned. Worthless thing. Should have taken me to Earth, but dumped me here instead. I kicked it into the ocean so no one would find it, but that didn't stop them from looking for me. Still don't know why I was being summoned." When a few moments passed without a reply, Theresa looked over.

Chabi stood frozen above the stove, paused in mid-motion. She sighed. "Summoned to Earth in a transpod?" She returned to her preparation, shaking her head. Then she threw a casual glance in Theresa's direction. "You're what—half-Terran, half-Equy? Thought so. No offense intended, so don't get your mane all in a tangle. Do you know how often they let non-Terrans ride in those things? More to the point, how often they summon non-Terrans to Earth in one?"

Theresa shrugged.

"No idea, eh? Suspected you didn't." The woman chuckled, pouring them each a cup from a whistling teapot. "Well, let me tell you a thing or two about those filthy Terrans. First, the transpod was the one technological edge that allowed them to overpower every inhabited world along the Perseus Arm without only a few serious fights. Their continuing dominance of that same expanse is made possible by their strict control of the technology. In other words—"

"If it gets out, they lose control of their Empire."

"Precisely. Now there are quite a few factions even among Terrans who believe they should lose control. They certainly proved pretty convincingly on Earth that they're incapable of managing their resources responsibly. Have you seen the place? Filthy is the least of it. No, no, no apology necessary. We deserve the epithet. And we'll make an Imperial mess of things along the Perseus Arm as well if we're allowed to. Just look at this planet. Benign species of hominid, a Sylvy race, just as yours is Equine, occupying a wet grassland world, and what do they do with it?"

Shrugging, Theresa sipped her tea, feeling the warmth reach her bones. Steam rose from her hide and dissipated.

"Enslaved the populace and put 'em to work in their smoke-belching factories, digging up the soil for the precious metals buried in the crust. And who profits from it?"

Theresa smiled across the top of her cup, content.

"Certainly not the Sylvy. Some corporate head back on Earth, and the shareholders of that same corporation, of course. After a few years of running this place, I was so disgusted with the oppression that I resigned in protest. Did a lot of a good, didn't it?"

The tea warm and her night among the Sylvy short, Theresa felt her eyelids slipping closed.

"Didn't matter that I had the Emperor's ear ..."

Theresa perked up. "Did you know he's dead?"

"By the moons of Cassiopeia, you don't say! Now, we're in trouble. Now, we'll see the extent of the Terran incompetence. Half the Perseus Arm held fast under the fist of an iron man, but without him—and with an heir who's all but an infant child—all I see is trouble ahead."

"What do you mean?"

"The Emperor Chingis Khan was not a man to leave much to chance. And he certainly wouldn't leave his Empire to founder in an interregnum. Not Chingis. The last time I saw him when I resigned in protest, he said, 'I'll be sending for you, you know. You may be leaving my service for now, but we both know you'll come back if I should but beckon.' And then he held up that silly amulet he always wore. 'Look for this,' he said, 'And then you'll know.' "

"Amulet?" Theresa asked. "What'd it look like?"

"I've probably said too much already. Gold rim, porcelain disk, a crystal of some type set in the center."

Theresa pulled hers from her pocket. "Like this?"

Chabi sighed. "I do stand corrected. Trouble is already here."

Chapter 5

"In the circle of thumb and forefinger."

Amber slid the amulet into place just as the first blast blew the nose off the ship next to hers. Flaming debris washed right through her fighter as though it didn't exist.

Engulfed by the explosion, and not understanding why it hadn't affected her, Amber slammed the controller forward, and the fighter leaped into space, leaving the burning hanger behind. She rocketed past the Imperial battlecruiser.

These controls look pretty simple, she thought, the brightly glowing amulet firmly in her left hand. The ship controller in her right, she tested. Left, right, forward, back with the controller. Roll left, roll right, dive, rise went the ship. Radio chatter from the pirate base rose in panic.

The center button must be the guns, she thought. A quick tap and a quick burst of fire. But how do I target? she wondered, looking around. Whatever way she moved her head, a red target appeared. Oh, easy! she thought.

Trained in hand-to-hand, Amber wasn't surprised how easily it came to her. The nuances would take time, she knew. Bringing the fighter around, she tried to assess the Imperial attack on the pirate base. Base chatter indicated the hanger had been leveled.

The heart of the battle was a confusion of blaster shots, the pirate base ablaze in five places. Two fighters launched from the battlecruiser and swung her way.

I've been spotted!

Amber launched her fighter at them, intuitively spinning to starboard. Her red target lit up and she fired, then spun to port while the fighter erupted in flames. The other fighter fell away to evade, and Amber followed, the other ship weaving out of her target sights. She broke off the pursuit, realizing that while she pursued this lone fighter, the battlecruiser was pounding the pirate base.

Five more fighters had joined the pursuit.

Amber gyrated through them, their blasts missing her, until one fighter remained between her and the battlecruiser. Her palms sweating, she clutched the amulet tightly and launched herself, blasters blazing.

She saw the bolt coming, thought, I'm going to die, oh, why am I trying to save these pirates I don't know, oh why am I…

The blast went right through her ship, and her, and kept on going.

Her rapid fire-blasters blew the fighter apart, and she strafed the battlecruiser from stern to bow.

A cheer went up on her com as she swung around for another run, Imperial fighters still trying to pepper her.

She took out one or two as she turned back, their shots passing right through her ship.

On her second strafing run, she targeted what appeared to be the bridge, the fuselage-mounted turrets tracking her, firing at will, but none of their shots landing. As she raked the behemoth vessel, explosions erupting with each strike, the battlecruiser turned slowly toward space, listing visibly, its hull aflame in thirty places, a thick, black plume of smoke in its wake, its agony all the more painful for its silence.

Amber came back around to pick off the fighters that had not broken off their bombardment of the rebel base, and just as she destroyed the last one, the dashboard warned of nearly depleted reserves.

Amber cursed her inability to pursue and destroy the battlecruiser and swung the fighter back to base. From above, she could see that half the buildings were ablaze, and the cratered surface was littered with bodies.

Keeping a tight grip on the amulet, she punched the com. "Reserves low, returning to refuel. And then I'll go get that blasted battlecruiser."

She brought the fighter down near the glowing remains of the hangar and leaped to the moon surface, her airshell wrapping her. The groundscrew hauled resupply lines over to the ship, shouting their congratulations to her over the optimitters. She stepped toward the hangar.

Beside the red-hot hangar doors stood Boss, the crippled cruiser just inside and what looked like a bundle of burnt rags beside him.

Boss looked at her. "She didn't have a chance."

"Huh?" Amber couldn't figure out what he was talking about.

He knelt beside the rags. "First blast caught her right away. Come on, help me out."

And Amber realized they weren't rags. "Minoa?" And she recognized the brown and white patchwork of the big-eared Canny. She probably followed me to the hangar, Amber thought, bending down to help him.

As they carried the Canny's body toward the big pile in the center of the pirate base, Amber's tears struck her airshell and sizzled away in a frozen mist.

Boss looked into the sky, toward the retreating battlecruiser, then brought his gaze to Amber's face. "Well fought, Amber Felly. You have the makings of a great warrior. In my youth I saw many battles, and I know you did your fighting with the help of something none of us has. And now I know how you arrived." He dropped his gaze to the pitted moon surface.

Amber saw even in the flickering light from the glowing rubble around them that he struggled mightily with himself. This can't be the first Imperial raid on his base, she thought.

"My name is Bati Kochakin. I was his majesty the Emperor Chingis Khan's Chief of Staff. I might have been at his side when he died." A single tear hit the airshell and dissipated in a cloud of glitter. "At his peak, just as he'd conquered the known worlds along the Perseus Arm, he decided to stop. No one, not even his closest intimates, knew why. After he changed, I found it increasingly difficult to work with him. He became moody, mercurial, even furtive. He'd always been suspicious of others and planned for the day that others betrayed him, but after that, it was ... it wasn't the same." He shook his head. "I begged his leave to retire, but he would have none of it. And then he began to disappear." Bati shook his head. "I don't know why I'm telling you this. You've been chosen. The whys and wherefores don't matter much. What matters is that you're here." He stopped and stared at her.

Confused, Amber shook her head. "But I don't understand. I'm not meant to be here. I was being summoned to Earth, and then the ... the transpod malfunctioned."

"No, it didn't," he said flatly. "It may have seemed that way. You were sent here. Given the one gift meant to tell me my help is needed. In Chingis Khan's Empire, there are no accidents, there are only his designs, oh yes, things that happen outside of his designs, certainly, but they're the rarities. He planned for this day. You didn't appear here on the day of his death by accident. What you did up there you didn't do by skill alone. You had help. Around his neck he always wore a small porcelain disk. Only half-a-dozen people knew what it did. I know that you have one. You couldn't have beaten off a battlecruiser in a fighter without one. I didn't know there were others. No, don't take it out, the others will see; avaricious eyes are all around. Tell me how you got it."

"It was given to me by my mother right before I left," Amber said. "She said, 'Your father wanted you to have this.'"

Bati frowned. "Who was your father?"

Amber shrugged. "Some Terran male she fell foolishly in love with. She never told me his name." She fingered the disk in her pocket, wondering if she should trust this Terran.

"You're wondering whether to trust me. All well and good. I'd be asking the same. Still want to get to Terra? Thought so. Ever been there? Thought not. I knew I'd be going back. I just didn't know the circumstances. I'd be honored to accompany you."

Amber felt as though she didn't have a choice. Terra was the mysterious Mecca, the terrible paradise that the Empire turned to for guidance and enlightenment. Dreaded but necessary, beneficent but despotic, magnanimous but capricious. A place so thick with bureaucracy that government-funded nonprofit bureaucracies helped people navigate its red tape.

Of course, she needed his help. Having been excoriated on Felly for being half-Terran, she could be certain of worse on Terra. Her being both an outlander and a member of the subjugated races would taint her as an object of scorn. Terrans were unlikely to acknowledge the Terran half of her. Then she smiled to herself. They've never seen a cat fight, she thought.

"Tell me what happened."

"Huh?"

"The day you left. Tell me what happened."

She recounted being in the commissary check-out line, being called the pejorative, the fight, the trip home, and the arrest. "They didn't seem much interested in prosecuting me. All they wanted was some way to deny that they'd willingly handed me over to the Terrans. So rather than enduring a trial and serving time, I said I'd go. And then my mother brought me this."

Bati shook his head. "Doesn't answer the most basic question. Why? Why here, why now, why you?"

Amber shrugged. "I don't know either."

* * *

"No, it's not by chance."

Kathy looked over at the Terran male, he who had known the danger the moment she'd appeared at his modest abode on the canyon rim, he who had ushered her into a ship and had launched moments before his home had been destroyed, he who had dodged and weaved and with her help had finally eluded their pursuers.

He who had led the assault on her homeworld, some twenty-seven years ago.

The two of them had found a ledge near the base of another canyon, the planet surface riven with cracks large enough to swallow whole cities, and they had slept, Kathy fitfully, the roar of ammonia-thickened water nearby, the constant crackling of her airshell as it fought off the noxious ammonia-laden atmosphere.

Although the sky was light, the canyon depths were still dark. She'd risen, found a private place for her toilet, feeling grimy with old sweat, growling pangs of hunger in her belly.

The airshell provided at least a semblance of heat, but it also emphasized her aroma. And Cannies were known for smelling bad if they didn't bathe.

He'd risen shortly afterward and had tinkered under the hood, the small scout looking no worse for wear for having nearly been blasted out of the sky.

Then he'd turned to her. "No, it's not by chance." No greeting, and not so much as a glance or a nod.

Rude people, these Terrans, Kathy thought, not quite sure how to respond. "My apologies for interrupting your life."

"You were intended to do so. No apology necessary."

Not a clue to the irony, Kathy thought. "Listen, Mengu, I'll find my own way to Earth, all right?"

He threw his head back and laughed. "How? By walking?" He laughed again and shook his head.

"Arrogant Terran! What do you know about it? We're going to get to Earth in that?" She pointed a sarcastic finger at his scout. "I'll get there faster by walking!"

He sobered up and regarded her thoughtfully, securing the engine housing. "Yes, you will—or at least as fast, since it's the transpod that'll get you there."

"What transpod?" Kathy was so startled that she looked around.

"The one you carry in the circle of your thumb and forefinger."

She'd heard him, but wasn't understanding. "What did you say?"

He smiled and leaned against the ship, the rock wall opposite them looking lighter. "Once you get there, what will you do? Ever been to Terra?"

"Transpod?" She lifted her left hand, the amulet nestled between thumb and forefinger. She closed the circle, and the rock walls shimmered as though insubstantial. "This?" She broke the circle, pulling her fingers apart, and reality around her snapped back into focus. "He did it!" she yelped. "He made it work! I'd read he wanted to condense the technology until it could be held in the palm, but there's nothing in the literature to indicate that he ever did!"

Mengu smiled at her outburst.

"That was how he conquered the Perseus Arm, wasn't it?"

"Conquering Earth itself—taming a world that had been at war with itself since a small community straddled the Tigris and Euphrates rivers—required far more than technological advantage. But yes, without it, Chingis would not have extended his reach very far."

"How did he do it? How did he put a transpod module into an object so small?"

Mengu shrugged. "The technical description is beyond my ken. Sounds as though you know the basics, yes?"

"The translation of space between multiple parallel universes, particularly ones traveling at different rates, where the passage of time differs from our own universe, each transpod able to translate its immediate surrounding space from one universe to the next and back, using the shifting tides between universes to move a transpod from one location to another."

Mengu nodded. "Much better than I could do. As to how he got a transpod into that—" He pointed at the amulet—"even more sophisticated."

"If the relativistic translation between universes holds, then so would the expansion and contraction across different gravitational densities, gravity being a function of distance and mass. If I were to transpod myself into the gravity field of a black hole, the transpod itself would translate the density appropriately, and I wouldn't feel any distress. It's only an untranslated gravity well that creates problems, since the density hasn't been translated. So that's how he did it, isn't it? He cross-translated a transpod unit to fit inside the crystal in the center."

"Sounds plausible, but then we have the anomalies."

"What anomalies?" Kathy saw the sunlight creeping down the opposite canyon wall.

"He kept the only microtranspod unit on his person," Mengu said. "He always wore it. Always. No one ever knew when he'd appear. He seemed to be everywhere at once, which was the substance of his power—his unpredictability. The minute a general rebelled or an enemy turned to do battle, there he was, right in front of them, attempting to persuade them to his side, or kill them on the spot. Moments before I launched the attack on the Canny homeworld, he suborned your leader and secured a victory. Our having demolished some of your outlying colonies certainly helped him press his case. And the Canny propensity for obedience was instrumental. Those obstreperous Fellies, won't obey their own leaders, won't even recognize when they're conquered. It's like herding cats! Anyway, he kept his transpod articulator on his person, the only one known to exist. Until now." Mengu nodded at her.

Kathy looked at the slim porcelain disk, the gold ring around the rim glinting in the morning light, the crystal in the center glowing with its own ethereal light. "So why me? And why now?"

"Precisely the questions," Commander Mengu Larine said.

* * *

"Precisely the questions," Chabi said, sipping deeply on her tea. "Why you? Why now?"

Theresa watched the Terran woman closely, wondering what the Emperor Chingis Khan had been like.

The old woman sat back. "He took his name from a fabled twelfth-century Mongolian warrior on Earth, a boy when his father was slaughtered in battle with a neighboring tribe. He took the reins of his tribe at fourteen, some legends say, and he conquered nearly a quarter of Earth's surface on the back of a—" Chabi lifted her gaze to look at Theresa and smiled—"of a horse."

Theresa giggled.

"Why you? Why now?" Chabi shook her head. "And why here?"

She might as well have said, "Why me?" Theresa thought.

"And why me?"

Theresa couldn't help smiling.

"You don't wonder at any of those things?"

Taken aback, she frowned. "Well, yeah, but …"

"Terrans send a transpod for a half-breed on a conquered world moments before the Emperor dies, a half-breed wearing an amulet identical to the one he himself always wore, and that transpod malfunctions and lands here, on this political backwater, within kloms of one of his closest political associates—the one who led the assault on your homeworld—and you don't wonder?"

"It does seem rather odd ..."

"Odd? Great galloping ghosts, girl! It was planned! Where did you get that, anyway?" She poked a finger at the amulet.

"My mother gave it to me just before I left, said my father wanted me to have it."

Chabi blinked at her. "Your father's a Terran? You're how old?"

"Twenty-seven."

Chabi looked at the floor and sighed. "I led the assault on your homeworld. We'd already demolished your outlying colonies throughout the Horsehead Nebula. I was poised with twenty legions of the most battle-seasoned Terran and Canny fighters—Chingis had conquered them some four years before, of course—each Terran fighter equipped with a transpod. You know he tried to persuade your leaders to submit, yes?"

"Persuade?! You mean he blasted apart our cities until we groveled?!" Theresa was suddenly furious.

"No, not what I mean at all. Sometimes he just used simple persuasion. Alliances, treaties, armistices, and even marriages were bargaining chips that he'd use to bring a world into his Empire. On one world, he fell in love with a king's daughter and asked for her hand in marriage. All he asked was allegiance. When the king refused, the Emperor ordered a broad-scale slaughter." Chabi looked at Theresa closely. "He tried honest persuasion with the Equy."

"Thank the universe, we didn't capitulate! Those slobbering Cannies, I swear, they're so obsequious—" Theresa put a hand over her mouth, wondering where that had come from.

"I wish he'd been successful," Chabi said quietly.

"But—" Theresa stopped herself, Chabi looking dejected.

"It was horrible."

She'd barely heard the older woman.

Chabi looked at her, tears streaking her face. "We slaughtered your people mercilessly. You didn't deserve that. We were wrong to do that. I don't know how you can ever tolerate my presence. I'm so ashamed!" Chabi dropped her gaze and began to weep.

In school, the Equy were taught about the heroic valor and sacrifice their forebears had exhibited in the war with the Terrans, their homeworld having held out for four months in the face of an inexorable onslaught, longer than any of the subjugated worlds except the Felly, who had resisted for six months. In the end, the Equy had fallen too, a quarter of their populace slaughtered, nearly all the breeding-age stallions dead.

And in the aftermath, Theresa's mother had fallen in love with one of the interlopers, and Theresa had been conceived.

"Somehow, he knew I was pregnant," her mother had told her once. "He came back only two weeks later, said he foresaw great things for you, told me he would provide for your future." Then her mother had turned away and had not mentioned it a second time. Theresa had been twelve then, had had her first menses, which had surprised her mother, Theresa significantly smaller than her peers. Only that once had Theresa gotten from her mother the sense of some deep, dark betrayal, perhaps the promise of providing for her future, a promise never fulfilled.

She'd forgiven her mother long before, knowing the horrific tragedy that had befallen her in the years before her conception, all her male relatives and all her male peers slaughtered relentlessly, and her stallion falling in the final battle.

Theresa looked at Chabi, who wept disconsolately at the destruction she'd wrought, and she found that it reflected the tragedy that her mother had endured on the other side of the same destruction—the loss of her stallion, the decimation of her people, and the subjugation of her homeworld.

And Theresa wondered, Why do we do these things to each other?

She sighed, knowing that the Felly and the Canny had fought like cats and dogs across the millennia, the space between their two constellations—the Cat's Eye Nebula and Canis Majora-Minora—littered with the detritus of a thousand battles.

"My apologies," Chabi said, her voice faint. "I know a thousand apologies will never be enough. After I slaughtered your people, I knew I couldn't continue serving him, and I asked Chingis permission to retire. He sent me here, hoping I might recover and return to serve him, but even here, I found conditions deplorable. I knew they were subjugating your peoples similarly, so I resigned even from this forsaken post. Now, he calls upon me from the dead to reenlist into his service, and I don't know why. You tell me you were summoned to Earth aboard a transpod, an honor never accorded to a member of the subjugated races. And instead of arriving there safely, you tell me it malfunctioned and landed you here."

Chabi looked at Theresa's left hand, the amulet cradled there, shaking her head in what looked to be disbelief. "There are no accidents. You're here by design, Theresa. Make no mistake.

"His design," Chabi said. "Always by his design."

Chapter 6

Amber Calico ducked, side-stepped, left, left, right, right, block, right, right, right, wove, and launched a left with all her might.

Her opponent teetered, the eyes unfocused, stunned at the speed of this smaller offworlder, and then she crashed to the canvas.

Amber danced back to her corner, her instinct to sink her fangs into neck to bite through spinal cord, a mouthpiece stopping her. A translator deep in her ear caught the referee's count.

The crowd was ominously silent.

Why did they cheer the last beating they witnessed? Amber wondered, having decked this opponent in the first half of the second round. Her coach had warned her not to move too fast, not to level her opposition so decisively, so early.

"They're here to see a good fight, not to see someone get savaged. Draw 'em out, make it last!" he'd shouted at her just before the match.

Maybe I just don't understand this sport, she thought, glancing over the crowd. Her fifth fight in two months since arriving on Earth, Amber had pulverized all her opponents, launching what she hoped would look like a legitimate career in this inhumane Terran sport called boxing. Bati Kochakin had helped her forge a resume of minor wins on the Felly homeworld and had gotten her a promoter and coach.

The crowd looked mean, ninety-five percent Terran, likely displeased to have watched one of their own get bombarded mercilessly by an offworlder Felly. The Terran had landed nary a punch.

Amber scowled at them while the referee counted down.

She felt no victory as she headed back toward the locker room, frustrated that she had to do this rather than what she wanted.

A door in the corridor opened. "What are you trying to do, eh?" The woman beckoned, the door behind her labeled, "Terra McFall, Welterweight Champion."

Bewildered, Amber followed.

The champion's dressing room looked like a posh place, silks and satins, rich woods and sparkling stones, plush and inlaid.

"Terra," the Terran woman said. "You're the Felly, aren't you?"

They were alone, Amber saw.

"I don't like the crew around just before a fight. After, when my brains are rattling in my head, I can't do without 'em. Let me see." Terran tilted Amber's head one way, then the next, turned it this way, then that. "Not a mark. Told the boys there wouldn't be. So, once again, what are you trying to do?"

Amber didn't quite know how to interpret the question. "I'm sorry, could you be more specific?"

Terra sighed. "Look, it's clear you can drop 'em in record time. Anybody can do that. But no one watching wants to see it. They aren't paying to see you pulverize somebody. They're here to see a fight, a contest, a match. You keep up like this, you won't get booked. The other managers won't put their kids in the ring 'cause they'll think you're just a hellcat bent on putting down anyone in your way."

"I'm not makin' a career of it," Amber said. "I got other skills."

"An' I don't? I ain't got what it takes to be Emperor. You?"

Amber shook her head, snorting. "Something to do until I get something else lined up."

"And just what else might that be? You don't look like most Fellies I've met. You part Terran? Thought so. Rare to see a half-breed. Didn't know they existed. Hey, don't take offense, none intended, all right? Just be careful, plenty in the crowd tonight who're purists—think of themselves as the master race, barely tolerate offworlders, consider mixes like you a sacrilege, abomination to be destroyed on sight. If you hadn't told me, I wouldn't know it. Keep it to yourself just to be safe, eh?"

Amber nodded, eager to get back to her locker room.

Through the walls a bell rang, and the crowd roared.

"I'm up when they're done. Keep it tight, kid." She chucked Amber playfully under the chin and opened the door.

What the hell was that all about? Amber wondered, the steam-stained walls and hard metal benches of her own locker room a far cry from the champ's.

Bati bustled in, looking nearly dejected in his somber, Earth-style clothes, his gaudy silks left behind on distant moons.

"Turn around," Amber said, shedding her robe to get in the shower.

His face in profile, eyes averted, he shook his head. "Nothin' new." While she'd pulverized her opponent, he'd been wandering Ulaanbaatar to find out who'd tried to summon her to Earth. In the three months they'd been on Earth, he'd found out little, except that the government was in an uproar, the succession in doubt, the infant son of the dead Emperor unlikely by most accounts to survive his infancy. "I swear this place has changed since I left fifteen years ago …"

Amber listened with one ear, the translator ear. She sighed and scrubbed, having heard his diatribe on the way things were at least a dozen times. Somehow, though, he'd always managed to return just as she was stepping in the shower. On Felly, she'd become accustomed to getting snubbed by the Toms, her Terran half making her too bulky to be attractive. On Terra, the opposite appeared to be true, her smallish frame attracting many a gander her way.

Out of the shower and into her clothes before he'd finished his ramble, Amber asked him about Terra McFall.

"This Welterweight Champ? What'd she say? Dumb as a brick but fights like a tiger. What're you gonna do, make this a career?"

"The way you're making progress, I'd better." Amber immediately bit her tongue. "Sorry, it's been difficult." She'd spent so much time hanging out in the gym, they'd dubbed her corner "the litter box." They'd been just as rude to her as her own Felly, but they'd shut up after the first fight.

Her "promoter," a nattily-dressed pitchman who'd only agreed to take her on when promised half her take, instead of the usual quarter, had only looked in on her once. He too had shut up after the first fight, watching her in wide-eyed wonder as she'd danced around her first opponent like a cat on a hot starliner hull.

Two months on this dirty grey ball, the air so choked with pollutants that everyone needed an airshell, the city of Ulaanbaatar considered one of the dirtiest. She was reluctant to visit any other city. Whatever "home" Earth might have been to these Terrans, they seemed to have gone to extraordinary lengths to foul their own nest. Amber was so frustrated and full of disgust that she'd been tempted to return to Felly after the first week.

"Someone went to great lengths to bring you here," Bati had reminded her. "It's no coincidence that the transpod malfunctioned. Someone else went to equal lengths to stop you and, I'm thinking, to pursue you. Imperial battlecruisers don't show up at pirate bases to make a social call."

"They came after me?" Amber had asked, wondering why anyone anywhere would go to such measures. Who was she? Just an offworlder half-breed ostracized by her own people, so utterly unimportant on her own planet that she'd hardly ever had a boyfriend, and at twenty-four, she counted herself lucky to have lost her virginity. "What use could they possibly have for me?"

"I know it's been difficult," Bati said, his face looking more worn than usual. "The pieces just don't fit, and I'm not getting the kind of help I thought I might." He looked around the dilapidated locker room.

Amber could see he wasn't seeing it.

"A transpod arrives on Felly, practically saves you from arrest and prosecution, the Emperor dies, and the transpod goes wildly off-course, to the very moon where I'd set up operations—me, a former battalion commander, then his Chief of Staff, one of the Emperor's favorites. I coulda been his prime minister! None of it occurred by chance. All by intent! But what intent? Whose intent? To what purpose? And what business does Chingis have in dyin' before he was supposed to? What gives him the right? I coulda been a prime minister!"

Amber could see how deeply hurt Bati was by the Emperor's untimely demise. Almost betrayed, she was thinking. How many other people had counted on the Emperor's living a lot longer? How many billions, even trillions of creatures, had come to like the peace that the Emperor Chingis Khan had imposed. The Fellies had come to like the welcome reprieve from constant war with the Cannies.

Amber's people had suffered terribly under the organized and concerted assaults that the Canny had repeatedly inflicted, and the Felly could never organize themselves well enough to conquer them completely. Only their vicious and crafty nature and their daring individual exploits had managed to keep the Felly homeworld free of the Canny leash. The Felly simply could not be leashed. The Terrans hadn't been able to leash them either, only to contain them. But in that containment, the Terrans had stopped them from warring on the Canny.

But now, the Emperor was dead, the succession in turmoil. And in that turmoil, the arrival on Earth of a half-Felly in the company of an elder Terran had gone unnoticed. The place was in an uproar. Every charlatan, trickster, politician, or CEO who thought he or she might profit from the impending change had also come to Earth. The influx had set off chaos on a scale that the planet was unprepared for.

Amber and Bati left the arena, their pockets lined, the need for entertainment such as theirs now at a premium, people's pent-up anxiety needing release.

The streets were thronged with people. Amber's incongruous appearance was masked under a low-brim hat, a long overcoat, and a wan moon. She'd gotten accustomed to the crackle of her airshell as it collided with other airshells, and with the enormous variety in the Terrans she passed. Shades from albino to deep, dark chocolate, shapes from nearly featureless to grotesquely prominent, Amber wondered at their propensity to call her Half-Breed.

Before you accuse me, she thought.

The capitol sky was filled with tubes—transtubes, watertubes, airtubes, fueltubes, electritubes. Only the waste tubes ran underground. Terrans never used transpods on Earth, she'd been told. With the advent of the frictionless surface, they'd devised an infrastructure that relied on means far less costly, and far less of a threat to their sovereignty than transpods—the pneuma tubes. They sent everything through tubes, even their information.

In between tubes, buildings soared into hazy skies, their sides slathered with advertisements—ever-changing screens flashing a visual cacophony to attract the slightly vagrant eye. Amber's brain had dulled to the profusion weeks before. If she looked too long, she got a headache.

While the airshell kept out most pollutants and much of the smell, Amber's ears could not suffer the overwhelming noise.

The translator in her ear blurting a series of syllables that might have been Felly but sounded like salad.

She'd detested this brash, chaotic world from the moment she'd arrived.

Suddenly, all the vidscreens changed, showing the Imperial crest.

"Your attention please. His honor, the Prime Minister of Mongol, Crybodan Occuday."

Movement at street-level stopped.

A face replaced the crest, high cheekbones over drawn cheeks, a long, sharp nose, eyes mere slits. "People of Mongol." The thin lips moved slightly out of time with the sound, the voice as clipped and precise as the face. "The untimely death of the Lord Emperor Chingis Khan has placed the succession of his heir Kublai Khan in doubt. To provide for a stable interregnum, to insure the succession, and to erase all doubt, the Imperial Administration has requested that I guide the realm until the Lord Heir Kublai Khan reaches adulthood. The Imperial Administration would not entertain even my most adamant of refusals, and so with great reluctance, I do accept this appointment and swear to abide by the Lord Emperor's will until his Heir comes of age, to rule the Empire with its interests close to my heart, and to hand over to the Lord Heir Kublai Khan, when he is ready to assume them, the reins of this great Empire."

The head bowed, and the Imperial Crest returned, which was soon replaced with the profusion of video, not of advertising, but of political commentary.

"That self-serving brigand!" Bati shouted, shaking his fist at the screen. "Who's the pirate now!"

* * *

Kathy Mongrel stepped slowly backward through the crowded assembly hall.

She had come for a lecture on Relativity Mechanics, the principles underlying the Transpod technology, and in the middle of the lecture by the wizened Terran, Professor Tossucan Aigar, renowned for his expertise in particle wave transmutation mechanics, the vidscreen had switched from his image to that of the Imperial Crest.

How dare they interrupt Professor Aigar's lecture, Kathy thought, indignant. This can't be good.

Just last night, listening to Commander Mengu Larine recount his continued frustration at the last three months without progress, Kathy had felt they might be reaching the limit of their resources.

Mengu and Kathy had come to Earth three months ago to try to find out who had summoned Kathy to Earth mere hours before the Emperor died. Despite three months in the Capitol, Ulaanbaatar, they'd found out nothing. A sprawling city that occupied an area about as large as the country it had once inhabited, Ulaanbaatar now sprawled across Mongolia proper and beyond. The desert that had seemed so bleak and lifeless, sandswept and sere, was now a solid megalopolis so weighted down by the heavy infrastructure needed to support it, that it was sinking slowly but surely into the earth. What had once been high mountain steppes were now sea-level sands, silted groundwater pumped out by the billions of liters per day.

Three months in the Capitol city had not impressed Kathy.

Overwhelmed, yes, but not impressed.

Mengu had begged an old associate to set them up on the university grounds, him as a janitor and her as a student. They occupied a decommissioned boiler room deep beneath the main university building, the entire school enclosed, inside its own dome, the grounds intricately and delicately landscaped, some of the flora and fauna extinct outside the university's protected environs.

On the two occasions that Kathy had left the University dome and entered Ulaanbaatar proper, she'd become so overwhelmed with the deluge of sight, sound, smell, and feel, that she'd nearly panicked the first time.

The second time, just last week, Mengu had given her something to help her relax, and then had taken her to see what she'd considered the most brutal sport she'd ever seen: Boxing.

Two Terrans pummeling each other half to death. Where was the fun in that? she'd wondered.

In the third to the last match, a Terran female had entered the ring against a Felly female—and had been flattened within minutes. Kathy had found herself on her feet, cheering loudly for the Felly, the only one in the crowd to cheer. In the third round, when the Felly floored the Terran female for the fourth and final time, Kathy hadn't dared to cheer, the mostly-Terran crowd grumbling at how swiftly and thoroughly the offworlder had beaten her opponent.

Mengu had ushered her out in the middle of the next match, his brusque manner conveying his displeasure.

"How was I supposed to know they don't like offworlders?"

Kathy's time was spent mostly in lecture halls such as Professor Tossucan Aigar's, taking classes in advanced physics, particle mechanics, and temporal theory. Mengu had helped her to fabricate a curriculum vitae, and had secured her a weekly, visiting-scholar lecture chair teaching post-grads the basics of transwarp timefolds, a topic in which she'd nearly received her doctorate before leaving the Canny homeworld. At thirty years old, Kathy carried herself with the aplomb of a post-doctorate fellow, despite having the bark of a post-adolescent punk.

At the back of the crowded assembly hall, Kathy looked over the disgruntled students, the university a hotbed of opposition to Imperial authority, what Mengu had more than once called, "Hot-aired revolutionaries."

In other words, Kathy and Mengu could expect no help from them. At his suggestion, she hadn't once implied to them she might be somewhat philosophically inclined to join them, despite her disgust with the way the Canny had capitulated en masse to the Terran onslaught without so much as baring a fang.

I'd better find Mengu, Kathy thought, seeing that Professor Aigar was shouting uselessly to an unlistening audience.

She slipped out the door and down the steps, tempted to drop to all fours and lope across campus to the main building. Too many people were rushing from place to place across campus, she saw. Of course, the announcement would cause turmoil. Of course, the Prime Minister's takeover would be met with dissension by student activists. But won't Imperial Forces be sent to places of likely opposition?

A familiar figure ran across the quad toward her.

Mengu!

He slowed and looked around as she approached. "This way!" and he gestured toward the nearest edge of the University dome. "We have to get out before they seal off the dome exits."

Unlike most of the city around them, the University lacked the dizzying overhead pipeworks—transtubes, watertubes, fueltubes, electritubes—all of its infrastructure underground. The underside of the dome was clearly visible through the canopy of tree, and the girders that held in place the thick plasma cap looked far too insubstantial to hold up such a large dome.

Mengu guided her toward the base of one of those girders, and there was no disguising its raw impressive bulk, the width easily thirty meters. An engineering marvel, the dome had been carefully constructed to balance strength and weight, the girders thinning as they arched toward the peak, the plasma they held aloft thinning also.

Several other figures hurried toward the exit, one of several exits at intervals around the base. Kathy wondered at their many furtive looks, as though they too suspected that the government might act.

"Why do I get the feeling this isn't welcome news?" Kathy asked as they neared the gate, walking just at his shoulder, her bulk matching his. Although there was a fair degree of sexual dimorphism among the Canny, the twenty-to-thirty percent larger mass of Canny over Terran cancelled any difference in size between Mengu and Kathy.

"No, it isn't," Mengu muttered, his gaze going back and forth. "Occuday is a snake, and he'll hiss in one person's ear while he rattles his tail in another's. He's not to be trusted with anything."

Kathy slid to a halt.

A battle-clad soldier stepped from the gate, behind him a slender woman in uniform. Her trousers flared just below the hips, her mighty breasts bedecked with medals. She looked right at Mengu.

"Commander Larine," she said, "you're under arrest."

* * *

Theresa Appaloosa lowered herself into the sewer, the thick miasma of Terran waste enveloping her like a cloud of poisonous gas.

She didn't know how much longer she could do this.

To her relief, the airshell kicked in and she took a deep breath. The indicator light on the belt was amber. I'll have to change the filter soon, she thought, her two-and-a-half months on the job unforgiving in its lessons. On her third day, the airshell had failed, its filters clogged, and Theresa had been deep in a culvert, the sludge around her boots oozing methane.

The knee-deep goop in this conduit had somehow gotten clogged. It should have been ankle-deep. Even the frictionless surfaces had not remedied the tendency for these waste pipes to clog.

Bent over, the ceiling low, Theresa slogged through the muck, the light on her helmet not able to pick out detail more than five meters ahead. If only I had a brighter lamp, she thought, sighing.

Knowing most clogs could be remedied with a shovel, she'd brought one and had secured it to the safety line, the cable snaking back out of the manhole she'd come through. Two coworkers stood ready to haul her up if she signaled distress.

What a lousy job, she thought for the billionth time, wishing Chabi would find out something soon. They'd been living in a tenement on the outskirts of Ulaanbaatar, Theresa going to work each day for the sewage reclamation district and Chabi making delicate inquiries amongst her old contacts for further information as to who might have tried to summon Theresa to Earth.

"No one seems to know anything," Chabi had complained frequently.

Theresa was happy to be doing something, disliking even a moment of idleness. Schlepping Terran waste wasn't quite the illustrious career she'd thought would bring her fame and fortune, but in the current circumstance, it was adequate. To keep herself busy in the evenings, she'd decided to take a class at the university, the basics of Transwarp Timefolds, taught by a visiting scholar, a droop-eared Canny.

The number of offworlders few, Theresa was even happier to have a mostly underground job, she and Chabi trying to keep their heads down. Finding a class taught by another offworlder had seemed a delight, but the boring Canny bitch just droned on and on, the Canny-Terran-Equy translation poor and the material difficult to follow.

Sighing, Theresa spotted an obstruction ahead.

The contraption clogging the pipe was unrecognizable. How someone had managed to get it into the sewer was baffling, the half-meter by quarter-meter frame too big to fit into any of the Terran-style waste receptacles she'd seen, which were difficult for her to use, their size typically too small for her sometimes large excretions.

Attaching the safety line through the loops on her belt, Theresa gave the line two sharp yanks to signal her coworkers, and then she headed toward the manhole.

Nothing happened. Two tugs was supposed to signal them to reel in the safety line slowly. Three tugs or frantic tugging—reel fast. One tug meant more line.

She gave the line two more sharp yanks.

Nothing.

Sighing, she made her way back toward the manhole. Looking up at the pie-sized slice of sky, she shouted, "Hey, guys, what are you doing up there?" She couldn't see anyone from where she stood, just the ladder and the safety line.

Disgusted, she climbed the ladder.

The crewhover sat there, cranes akimbo, but no crew.

Looking around, she caught a glimpse of a vidscreen. The translator in her ear non-directional, she couldn't quite make out what the newscaster was saying.

Waste still sloughing off her chest-high coveralls, Theresa looked beyond the yellow tape and hailed a passerby. "What are they talking about?"

The poor fellow caught one glimpse of her and almost needed a waste receptacle. He hurried away without answering.

She ducked under the tape, the Terrans scattering at the muck-slathered Equy, and stepped toward the vid blaring over the walkway.

"The Prime Minister's surprise announcement a few minutes ago brings with it the certainty of a smooth succession and a great relief to the Empire as a whole." The commentator stuck a microphone into someone's face. "Doesn't Prime Minister Occuday's Regency during the Crown Prince's minority bring you a sense of peace?"

The Terran's eyes were wide as moons and his face pale as a cloud. "Uh yes, yes, of course, of course it does. I feel much more secure." The Terran wiped the sweat from his forehead.

The newscaster's face came on again. "There you have it. Just moments after the announcement by the Prime Minister, Cyrbodan Occuday, that he reluctantly accepts the title of Regent until the Heir, his majesty Kublai Khan, comes of age, citizens around the Empire are already looking forward to the prosperity that his Regency will bring. For more on the tranquility that we can all—"

Theresa snorted and stepped back to the crewhover. She didn't need to be told what to expect. The tenor of the people shuffling past the worksite was enough, their furtive glances and fear-filled faces telling her everything. She frowned at the crewhover, still without its crew. She had the feeling she wouldn't be missed. Stepping out of the excrement-covered waders, she hurried away, heading for the tenement flat that she shared with Chabi.

Her airshell blinked to red and collapsed just as she reached the intersection near their building. Standing half in a doorway so she didn't get jostled by the crowd, looking down at her waist, Theresa quickly changed battery and filter. Reminding herself to charge it when she reached the flat, she looked up.

A trio of uniformed goons emerged from the tenement entrance, dragging Chabi.

Theresa pressed herself back in the doorway. Even from this distance she could see that Chabi was studiously not looking in Theresa's direction.

They threw Chabi in the back of an unmarked hover and took off.

Theresa glanced up at the window, where she'd often sat and watched the teeming city below.

A Terran face now did the same.

She pulled back into the doorway before the eyes found her.

Heart thundering in her chest, Theresa wondered, what now?

Chapter 7

Heart thundering in her chest, Amber wondered, what now?

On the way to the grimy, one-room rental flats beside each other on the sixth floor of a vermin-infested hotel, Amber and Bati had gotten separated. A block away, she'd stopped to admire a street vendor's drawings. The vendor, without her knowing it, had whipped out a portrait of her with a poverty of strokes, and presented it to her for sale.

She'd laughed at the caricature, but her laughter had died when shouts from down the street caught her attention.

"No, don't turn around," the sketch artist had said, the smile never leaving her face.

Amber had obeyed, her pulse racing.

"The Imperials asked about him earlier, the old man you're with. They didn't ask about you, an' I didn't tell 'em."

They'd thrown Bati in the back of a hover.

"Probably taking him to Intelligence," the sketch artist had said.

Now, a glance at the sixth-floor window showed a suit in dark glasses scanning the street below.

Amber quickly walked the other way, trying to keep her pace leisurely, her heart thundering so loudly she was sure they heard it even from that distance.

Again, she wondered, what now?

Two blocks down, she stopped in a doorway to see if she were being followed. No suspicious characters. Even so, she circled the building and crossed the grassy median, then circled that building.

Would I know if I were being followed? she wondered, looking both ways from the night-darkened doorway.

A figure came around the corner, an easel over one shoulder, a portfolio in the other hand, her drab dress swaying. The sketch artist kept her head low, her dark curls falling around her face.

She stopped opposite Amber. "Follow me," said the low voice, nary a look in Amber's direction.

Cold and feeling forsaken, Amber did so, despair beginning to set in, her one guide now gone, and only an unknown, unobtrusive street vendor to trust.

Amber stayed across the street, passersby infrequent and seeming preoccupied with their thoughts, none of them looking at her or even seeming to notice. She walked several blocks, trailing the sketcher fifteen to thirty meters, the hunched figure with an easel over the shoulder never looking to see if she were there.

I don't even have a place to live, she thought, Bati having secured that. Her Terran rudimentary and the eartrans unlikely to last forever, Amber wondered how she would manage to navigate this dark, forbidding planet and these dark, foreboding people.

The sketcher turned into a building that looked in little better shape than the vermin-infested hotel where she and Bati had rented rooms.

Amber found her just beyond the vestibule.

"Beatrice—but you can just call me Betty. Come on." And Betty gestured up the stairs. Whatever palsy or infirmity that had caused the woman to bend over seemed not to afflict her now as she bounded up the stairs two at a time, seeming unencumbered by portfolio and easel.

Amber followed her up three flights of stairs.

Betty led her to a door and let the both of them in, then gestured silence, motioning Amber to stay just inside the door. Betty then looked in the other room, went to the window and threw it open, put her hands on the sash and stuck her head out as far as she could without losing her balance, her airshell crackling against the noxious air.

Pulling herself back in, Betty sighed, looking relieved. "I had to make sure we weren't followed. Let me get us some tea. You'll have some, yes? Thought so. Have a seat, rest your paws, must be worried about your friends, no, no, all in good time, rest yourself, go on."

Amber sat, Betty nearly pushing her into the chair.

Sketches festooned the walls, not a single space clear. While Amber watched, Betty stuck her portrait beside that of Bati, a quadtych of others beside them. The furniture was simple, threadbare cloth stretched over limply-stuffed cushions, a lamp with a shade askew, a large, stationary easel beside the window, a half-finished sketch of a distant building sketched onto paper.

Betty bustled over to the kitchenette—a wall devoted to food preparation, but otherwise as much a part of the main room as the threadbare furniture. "Been watchin' you two since you arrived, thought it was odd to see an old Terran with a young Felly at a seedy downtown hotel. You know those places are infested with vermin? Drug dealers, pickpockets, scam artists, narcotraffickers, shellgamers, and the like? And that's just the insects!" She threw her head back and laughed. "Saw the Imperials appear this morning after you'd both left, knew something was up. Isn't everyday the Prime Minister announces he reluctantly accepts the Regency. Sending his goonsquad after you, now that's a bit of a puzzler, it is." Betty tossed pots about, as though digging for something. "Here it is, it is." She pulled out a teapot. "Doesn't surprise me that he'd try to silence all dissidents, it doesn't. Must be a hundred thousand in Ulaanbaatar alone, and several million on Earth. Part of it's the show, you know. Silence them publicly, and your other opponents will keep quiet. Now you—" she leveled a finger at Amber—"are another bit of mystery. What possible reason might prompt Bati to reconnoiter in a seedy hotel for three months with you? At first I thought he'd brought a plaything—now don't take offense, as the place has quite a few amusements of similar type available—but I could tell it was something else." Betty brought a cup of tea.

Amber cradled it, enjoying the warmth. "He wouldn't be here if I hadn't asked for his help."

The eyes alighted on her face, the thoughts apparent.

"You're surprised. You thought he was here because of the Emperor's death?"

"Everyone else did too." Betty shrugged. "Bewildered his tails when he went to the gym most nights."

Amber realized Betty knew more than she'd been letting on, the warm cup of tea no longer a comfort.

"I sketch everybody, and ask a lot of questions, too. Don't worry about me. If I've got an ambition, it's to draw the next Emperor, a simple if impossible wish. That, and keep my nose in the air for the next change on the wind." She glanced at the portrait of Amber that she'd just hung. "See those other four? Arrived the same day you did. Know who they are? Didn't think so. The top one, next to the Canny, Mengu Larine, Lieutenant Colonel, fifth division commander of His majesty's Navy, led the assault on the Canny homeworld. The side one, beside the Equy, Chabi Schahahaday, two-star General, third and sixth division of his majesty's Navy." Betty swung her gaze to Amber. "And beside you, Bati Kochakin, Chief of Staff, presumed the next Prime Minister, Chief negotiator in the armistice that ended the Felly standoff. Your people gave Chingis the toughest fight he'd had, by the way. You gave him such a fight that he was ready to annihilate your people. Bati negotiated the containment just in time.

It would have been a pyrrhic victory if Chingis had wiped you out, you know."

Amber sipped, steam shrouding her face and moistening her whiskers. "All the same day?"

"All of 'em arrived the same day—one day after the Emperor dies. Not a coincidence. I don't know what it means, except maybe Chingis reaching out from the grave. Unlike him to leave his succession in doubt."

"I hear he was a careful man."

Betty snorted. "Not how I'd describe him. Bold, brash, daring—but all intentional and always with a larger purpose in mind. I don't think he left his succession in doubt at all." She turned to look again at Amber. "I think we're all strands in his web. Especially you six." Betty gestured at her sketches.

Bewildered, Amber shook her head.

"I can't piece it together, either." Betty sighed and stood. "Couch is yours for the night. Can't have you stay longer."

"I don't want to stay even that long, my apologies. I appreciate your company, and you've been so kind and generous, but I don't want to endanger you further. All I really need to know is where they've taken Bati."

"What good would that do you? He'll be wrung dry of information and killed. Occuday won't leave that to chance."

"I have to get him out."

Betty stared at her. "Don't know the impossible when it bares its claws at you, eh?" She nodded and reached for her sketchpad. A few rapid swipes and she ripped the page off in Amber's direction. The rudimentary map showed a building complex several kilometers away, if the scale was accurate. "That's the Khochakin Fortress, impossible to penetrate." Betty smiled. "The couch is yours if you've a mind for it."

"Thanks." Amber folded the map and took her leave, liking Betty.

* * *

Kathy panicked and clutched the amulet in her pocket.

Reality shimmered and grew fuscous, as though a cone of tinted plasma had enveloped her.

"Where'd she go?" the beefy armed soldier said.

"Take the traitor to holding," the uniformed woman said. "I want a perimeter. She has to have gone somewhere!" She pushed her face into Mengu's. "If this is one of your sly tricks, I'll slice off your balls! Where'd she go?" she snarled.

"Where'd who go?" Mengu snarled back.

She brought her knee up, and Mengu crumpled.

Kathy turned away, her stomach in knots.

They dragged him, still balled up and clutching his groin, through the door and out of the University dome.

Kathy followed, the sensation of moving through solid objects disconcerting. They loaded him into a hover, and she managed to slip into the back through the reinforced rear compartment wall.

The hover hummed to life and lifted.

Had she not been an engineer, she might have wondered how the hover had lifted her. Knowing its interface provided some integration with the current space-time universe, the transpod technology allowed a person to move in relation to exterior objects directly under that person. Kathy hadn't yet figured out how to override that function, which would have enabled her to float weightlessly. The theory of multiple parallel universes posited that light, gravity, and time all derived their existence from being, and that each possessed properties of both particle and wave. In their transition from particles to wave and back, called interstitial mechanics, light, gravity, and time all emitted a field—much like a magnetic field—that influenced surrounding parallel universes. The interception of these interstitial fields allowed Kathy to perceive one universe while standing entirely within a closely-aligned parallel universe, the amulet having embedded in its crystal core the electronic interface that broadcasted the interstitial field from parallel universes. Hence, she could see, hear, and feel the parallel reality while someone in that reality would be unable to see, hear, or feel her, unless they too were using an interstitial field translator, or IFT.

Kathy wondered whether to kill the IFT so she could tell Mengu she was there. We're probably on vid, she thought, deciding against it. The police hoverwagon was large enough to hold twelve prisoners, six on each side, Mengu the only occupant. His head hung between his knees, he looked dejected, as though he'd given up hope.

"Don't give up!" she wanted to shout, but she knew he couldn't hear her. What can I do? she wondered, seeing through the narrow window that the hover approached a compound with multiple layers of fence, gnarled strands of wire looped through the tops, spotlights raking the night like knives.

Sweat beaded on her forehead. Despite the ferocity of the Canny people, Kathy had always pushed herself to excel academically. A fighter she was not.

I have to know where they're taking him! she thought, steeling herself and forgetting momentarily they didn't know she was there.

The hover settled behind multiple fences, and the doors swung open. Two soldiers leaped right through her, grabbed Mengu and dragged him onto the landing pad.

Startled, Kathy fell off the hover through the side wall. Scrambling to her feet, she stood to her full height.

"What was that?" one guard said, the circle of guards looking in her direction.

The little contact she did have through her feet must have alerted them. She held still, trying to make herself as small as possible.

"Hearing things again, Muchaca? Lay off those drugs, eh? Let's get him stripped."

They pulled all his clothes off, leaving Mengu on the hoverpad naked, and went through each piece of clothing thoroughly, as though looking for something.

His face that of an old man, his body looked but middle age, his abdomen rippled, pectorals prominent. In good shape for a codger that old, Kathy thought.

"That everything?" The commander with the bullet breasts held a handful of objects, money, a locket, an identicard. "Get his clothes on, and take him to interrogation." She strode off toward the building, glancing again at the objects in hand.

Tempted to follow, Kathy stayed with Mengu.

They took him to a room bare of comfort, a chair, table, and lamp the only objects, and left him propped in the chair. Three walls were covered with mirrors.

He sighed and leaned back in the chair, shielding his eyes from the one bright light.

Kathy decided to do a little exploring, making sure to note his exact location in the building. The amulet clutched tightly in her left hand, she moved through walls easily, but had to look through each wall lest she accidently step off into an open stairwell or elevator shaft.

The lower floors seemed crowded with prisoners—newly arrived prisoners, in bare rooms with iron-barred cubes constructed right inside them, cells looking hastily confabulated. Guards everywhere, she stumbled across two other interrogation cells, one with an older man with thick black ringlets falling nearly to his waist, the other holding an iron-haired woman of small stature. Like Mengu, they occupied rooms devoid of comfort and mirrored on three sides.

On the next two floors were workcubes, their chairs empty at this time of night, except for a lone soul or two.

On the fifth floor, activities were rampant, aides scurrying between cubes, and at one end, a gathering of elaborate uniforms and luxuriant suits.

Including the commander of the unit that had apprehended Mengu, her slim figure and pointy breasts the draw of many a glance from her male and female peers. Her trousers flared just below her hips—like riding breeches, Kathy thought, wondering at the affectation.

"Nothing!" she shouted at them all. "Not a single suspicious item among their possessions! Secretary Baihatu, I'm afraid your intelligence must be faulty. These three decrepit outlanders don't appear to have a single transpod controller between them!"

A suited gentleman with bristling sideburns shook his head. "You didn't look hard enough, Commander Tureg. I suspect you neglected body cavity searches and molecular scans. Ah! As I thought. Remember they're from the old regime. They resigned before our late Emperor grew soft. These are crafty people, these three. Get to it! Find those controllers!"

Her porky breasts seemed to deflate. She shot a look at a subordinate. A man ran off. "Let's hope you're right, Secretary. Otherwise, we've captured the wrong people."

"How could those three half-breeds have obtained transpods, unless given them by these three expatriates? You know how rigorously we control them." The sideburns bristled even more. "Former high officials—I'd be surprised if they didn't abscond with transpods when they resigned, but one of the conquered peoples having one? Impossible!"

The commander stepped close to the Secretary, the metal band on her arm etched with a Terran hand, palm out. "What about those strikes that Prime Minister Occuday ordered? Just like him to withhold such important information, eh?"

Kathy had to step close to hear what they were saying.

"Doesn't it fit? He orders a single thermoprotonic strike on each homeworld of the Felly, Canny, and Equy, and then these three turn up here on Earth within a few days, each of them with a half-breed in tow—a Felly, a Canny, and an Equy. I'm telling you, Secretary, I think we've got the wrong people."

"Uh, er," the Secretary said, looking around. "Did you hear something?" He shuddered visibly, a gleam of sweat on his forehead. "Thought someone was right there for a moment." He pointed right at Kathy.

Her snout already moist with sweat, Kathy got more nervous and took a step backward, a big drop of sweat leaping from her snout in slow motion and hitting the carpet with a splash.

"What's that, there on the floor?"

* * *

Theresa clutched the amulet, peering around the corner.

The dim, wide corridor appeared empty, the half-height doors equally spaced on both sides, their upper halves all open. The straw-covered dirt floor looked as though it would be silent enough.

Theresa yawned. She'd been up all night, wandering Ulaanbaatar aimlessly, worried sick about Chabi and wondering where they'd taken her, feeling helpless and adrift, alone now on an alien world.

Walking past an oval stadium, she'd smelt a whiff of straw, the filters on her airshell faltering. A more pleasant aroma than most she'd encountered, Theresa had found her way to a long shed to one side of the large oval, a shed open at either end, large bales stacked near the entrance.

Though somewhat dry, the straw had been delicious. Eating her fill, Theresa had then looked into the shed, her appetite sated, her eyelids heavy.

A roan male whinnied, his head protruding from the open top of one half-height door, "Hey, Beautiful."

She heard both the original speech and the translation through her earpiece, the sounds oddly similar. "Hey, Handsome." Perhaps it was her fatigue, or Chabi's detainment, or her having eaten her fill, or just the sight of someone having a familiar aspect and speaking an almost comprehensible tongue. She was out of her formalls and into his stable before she could think.

She swam up through sleep at someone's nudging her and she tried to tell them to stop but all she could do was mumble.

"Wake up!"

The shove was hard enough to hurt and she complained," Ow!" and rolled to her feet.

The stallion nickered at her and shouldered her to the door, where she took a moment to don her formalls, half aware of where she was, dreamily immersed in paroxysms.

"Oh, hello," said a male voice. A small man stood there, his eyes wide, a thick bundle of straw in his arms.

"Pleased to meet you, I'm Theresa." She stuck out a hand.

He shook, but kept ahold of it. "A hoof! You really are an Equy. Never met one. Pleased! I'm Jiminu—call me Jimmy for short. Got some straw in your hair, looks like you been rollin' in it. Spend the night in Emperor's stall? He's a gentle one. Generous in many ways, but I guess you found that out, didn't you?"

"Uh, yeah," Theresa said, sure he could read her mind, the memory of Emperor's generosity sending a fresh gush of warmth through her. She was glad the formalls were waterproof. "He was very nice, Jimmy. Bringing him breakfast? The straw's a bit on the dry side, by the way."

He let go of her hand finally. "It is?" He looked at Emperor. "That right? A bit dry for you, Old Emp? See if we can get some a bit more moist." He smiled at her. "We'll be studding him out later today. He's downright majestic, just like his name. I understand the males of your species are similarly proportioned. Oh, uh, sorry, didn't mean to embarrass you. Anyway, boss catches you here, he'll turn you in. Better get goin', miss Theresa."

She put a forlorn look on her face and told him she didn't have anywhere to go.

"Uh, can't say here in the stables, but..." He looked both ways along the stable corridor, then tossed the hay in with Emperor and gestured her to follow. "You gotta promise you'll go tonight, all right? Not supposed to do this. Can't make any noise all day either, all right? This way."

He led her between two stalls to a larger shed connected by a breezeway. Bales were stacked to the ceiling.

"Climb up there, I'll bring you some lunch if'n you're wanting something beside straw. Yeah, up there. No one can see you from down here. The place is crawling with Imperials—Prime Minister coming to the track tonight or something, so stay real quiet."

Theresa didn't need to be told twice. She lay down just a few feet under the rafters and was instantly asleep.

Chapter 8

Waiting outside the compound, yawning terribly, Amber decided to return to Betty's for some sleep, the multiple fences of razor-topped wire looking impenetrable.

A hover came over the roofs and settled into the compound.

I really should go before someone spots me, Amber had been thinking, crouched in a doorway, her dark brown formall blending in with the door behind her, the hood pulled far forward over her head like a cowl, pretending to sleep. The eastern sky held a hint of blue.

Her irises wide, she tracked the hover as it floated to the ground, where five Imperials got out and surrounded the rear doors. Two of them went in and extracted a small, almost-elfin Terran, a female.

From her point of view, at least a hundred meters away through three layers of fence, Amber couldn't see clearly what they were doing.

After a few minutes of bustling, they took the woman inside.

The amulet between her fingers, Amber wondered. It would be so easy to walk right in there. She slipped it back into her pocket before she did something rash.

A Canny appeared down the street, walking furtively toward her.

Where'd she come from? Amber wondered, instantly bristling. The Cannies had been enemies of the Felly for centuries. Amber feigned sleep as the Canny walked past, the dog-faced bitch seeming preoccupied with the fenced compound, glancing that way even as she continued far down the street.

Bleary eyed, Amber rose and slinked away, taking an alley back the way she had come. Her sense of direction poor, she was soon lost, and the rudimentary map that Betty had drawn was no help.

She balled up the map and hurled it against the wall, anxious with the brightening sky behind her, frustrated and despairing.

* * *

What now? Kathy wondered, pacing the street outside the secure complex where Mengu was being held.

And probably tortured.

Her fingers securely around the amulet, Kathy had fled the command center, not waiting around to find out what they might have seen through the interstitial fields masking her presence, not wanting to risk discovery.

Kathy passed a doorway where she belatedly realized someone was sleeping, her nose detecting faster than her eyes that the person was Felly.

Thankfully, she'd already passed the doorway, her people having warred for centuries with the Felly. Kathy kept an eye over her shoulder as she continued pacing, Fellies known for their wiliness and ferocity in single combat.

The perimeter of the compound was the same at all points except one: three gates, one inside the other, each with enough space in between to close the first gate before the second opened. The hover she'd arrived in had simply flown over the fences.

Kathy kept her collars up and her head low as she passed, giving no indication she noticed anything. How can I get Mengu out? she wondered.

The amulet was secret, of course. She and Mengu had used it to escape from the Imperial attack on his compound, and then had come to Earth with it as well, enabling them to arrive undetected. Mengu had first alerted her to its powers, but when asked later, he'd been unable to tell her what they were.

He'd also realized that he'd pointed his escape shuttle right at a canyon wall with the belief that she'd known how to use it. "I almost painted the wall with our ship."

With little knowledge of how to use it, Kathy was reluctant to extract Mengu from the compound. She was sure she could do it, but her doing so would cause such an immediate uproar that they would end up having nowhere to go.

Mengu's detainment on the heels of the Prime Minister's announcement was certain to have been intentional, the new Regent consolidating his power and squelching any possible opposition. They must have known we were here, Kathy thought, wondering why they'd waited until the announcement itself.

Perhaps if you're not the Regent, you can't issue such orders, she thought.

Feeling the porcelain disk in her pocket, she wondered how to unlock its power. The Emperor Chingis Khan had conquered the Perseus arm with an identical device and armies equipped with transpods, she added, reminding herself she didn't have an army to back her up. But Kathy remembered the legends of Emperor known to be "everywhere at once."

Come on! she told herself, figure it out! The three basic components of the universe—time, mass, and distance—merely three articulations of the same thing, each with properties of particle and wave, each transition between particle and wave creating interstitial fields between parallel universes. The basic principle of transpod technology posited that the transition of each component could be utilized to transport a person to a parallel universe by interpolating the interstitial fields.

The reason I can coexist in the same room with people who can't see me is that I'm viewing their interstitial field from a parallel universe, but I'm using the interstitial light field. How do I use the interstitial time and distance fields?

Frustrated that she couldn't access the other two components of the interstitial transpod technology, Kathy kept walking, no clearer on what to do.

Giving her mind the illusion of action simply by walking.

She left the compound and strode toward the rising sun. Or the direction she thought it should be. The tube-strewn urban canopy begrudged her any glimpse of the mustard-brown sky.

Great God of Dogs, I hate this place!

* * *

Theresa woke with a start, the voices in her dream continuing below.

The roof girders right above her, she lifted her head carefully to peer over the bale to the straw-covered floor below.

"... Looking worn today. That jockey hasn't been studding him out behind our backs, has he? Just like Jimmy to play us, the weasel!"

A man and a woman conversed in low tones below her, beside them a short, gray-furred figure. The man was instantly recognizable—the Prime Minister, Cyrbodan Occuday. He wore a long cape, held closed at his throat by a clasp.

Jimmy mentioned he'd be here, Theresa thought.

"I assure you, Sire, if he is, I'll find out," the woman said.

"What about you? Why don't you ride? Old Mongol tradition dates back twenty-five hundred years. No, I know, not for everyone. What'd you get from our three prisoners?" The clasp at his throat was a porcelain disk rimmed with gold, at its center a crystal.

Fear seized her. Her hand went to the disk in her pocket. Her fingers closed on the crystal, finger and thumb pinching the stone between them.

Silence fell.

She frowned, the crystal warm between forefinger and thumb.

The three figures below looked frozen, the absolute dead silence eerie.

She unpinched her fingers.

"Well, Sire, they're pretty cagey, tough old birds with hides thicker than leather. They don't feel pain like most people."

"What did you find among their possessions?"

"Searched 'em thoroughly, nothing unusual. One had a locket." The woman pulled out a heart-shaped object on a chain.

The man took it from her. "Bati always wore it." He dropped it on the ground and crushed it under his boot. "Nothing else?"

"No, Sire." Although small, the woman exuded power and discipline, her uniform immaculate, the metal band on her arm etched with a Terran hand, palm out, medals cascading in neat orderly rows at the left breast, her ample mammaries as proud as missiles. "What were you looking for?"

He fingered the clasp. "Something to indicate why they're here. They must know I won't abide their meddling. It's not just by chance they arrived simultaneously. They must be plotting something."

"But they've left their allies behind. Stupid to have come without reinforcements. Why do you suppose they did that?"

"That's what's got me worried. They don't seem to have been in contact with each other. What have you found—"

Theresa pinched the crystal again. Sorry to interrupt you, Prime Minister, Sire, Sir, she thought.

The three figures below her, stone still, looked comical. Beside the Terrans stood a gray creature, just over three feet tall, whiskers twizzled skeptically, its small eyes on either side of the conical snout almost ludicrous, and its long gray tail laid out on the straw behind it like the trail of a long evening gown.

Grinning at the two Terrans and curious at the gray offworlder rodent, Theresa climbed down the bales, carefully keeping the crystal pinched between her fingers. They remained frozen, all three, the silence thick. Theresa couldn't even hear the sound of her own feet.

The gray offworlder looked like one of the ubiquitous Murry, a conquered race that had not only capitulated to the Terran onslaught but had hurled itself en masse upon its collective belly to prostrate itself before the new oppressors. The Murry had then set about making its peoples indispensable to the new regime, becoming personal slaves to the Terran oligarchy and ingratiating themselves so thoroughly that having an obsequious rodent at one's beck and call had become de rigueur for the Haute Culture.

Theresa stepped up to the Prime Minister and examined his clasp closely.

Identical to the amulet between her fingers, except for the clasp attachment. An orange point of light at the rim appeared to be the only difference.

Didn't I see the Emperor wearing one?

She looked at the amulet between her fingers, certain it had frozen the two people and one offworlder in mid-conversation.

And was startled to see an orange point of light near the center, a millimeter from the crystal embedded in the porcelain disk.

Not knowing what to think, but not wanting to get caught and not knowing how long the amulet would hold them immobile, Theresa knelt and picked up the crushed locket, then stepped from the shed into the breezeway.

The mid-morning sun was warm and cheery, if masked by the usual thick, brown haze. She stepped toward the open corral, a withered tree just beyond the chest-high fence. Under the tree, she stopped.

A leaf hung in the air, suspended by invisible means.

Alarmed, Theresa looked around. Beyond the corral, fifty meters away, was the racetrack. On a horse in mid-stride was Jimmy, his feet in the stirrups, his backside in the air, his right arm back and up, a riding crop poised. A spray of dirt hung suspended behind a hoof just leaving the dirt.

She made her way over to the track, looked around the deserted spectator stands to make sure no one was looking, and took her fingers off the crystal.

Jimmy galloped on past, crop flying.

What is this thing? Theresa wondered, quickly tucking the amulet into her pocket.

She leaned against the fence and watched Jimmy ride around the track.

He slowed to a trot as he approached her. "The boss doesn't like spectators, ma'am. I'm gonna have to ask you to leave. Sorry about that."

"So am I," she replied. "I'd love to take a ride."

"The boss doesn't let anybody but me ride his horses."

"I wasn't talking about the horse."

"Look, you gotta leave," he said loudly, his face beet red. "But come back tonight," he added more quietly.

"How do I get out of here?" She grinned and went to way he pointed.

Grubby, tired, hungry, and now alone, Theresa found her way to the street, the crowds not as thick here near the stadium. She looked up into the tube-strewn sky and wondered, What now?

Chapter 9

"Look, I really need some help," Amber said.

The Welterweight Champ glanced over from the shadow she was boxing without interrupting her routine. Sweat sprayed from her arms with each punch, the sequence so rapid only a trained eye might follow.

But Amber's eye was trained. "That was the pattern you used to knock out the last contender."

Terra stopped in mid-punch. "You have a suggestion?"

"Your opponent can picked apart the pattern, expose its weakness, and exploit it. But you're the champ, not me."

The boxer launched into another fusillade, sending off more spray. "Wait for me in my locker room."

Amber grinned. She wasn't sure Terra McFall could do anything for her. Waiting in the Champ's silk-curtained, satin-walled locker room, Amber couldn't have said why she'd come, except that she didn't have any place else to go.

In the middle was a massage bench, waist-high, thinner than most massage tables, the welterweight quite slender. Amber lay down, thinking, I could use a massage right now.

The hot breath in her ear woke her, and the sweaty face just centimeters from hers was full of mischief. "You need a shower as much as I do." And Terra kissed her.

Behind Terra, steam billowed from a hot shower. The Champ wore only an inviting smile.

Later, wearing a jumpsuit she'd borrowed from Terra, Amber looked at herself in the mirror. Red stripes with interwoven glitter traced lines down her arms and thighs, a similar band around her waist emphasizing her bust.

"Thank you," Terra breathed into her ear, cupping her breasts through the fancy jacket.

Amber moistened at the touch, the memory of Terra's body and attention nearly causing more contractions.

"You look lovely," Terra said, stepping back.

"I feel lovely," she said, smiling shyly at her. She turned in front of the mirror. Emblazoned across the back in interwoven glitter was "Terra."

"Be back in a moment." Donning her robe, Terra peeked both ways out the door before stepping into the corridor.

Admiring herself in the mirror, Amber looked into her own face, bemused at her behavior. She'd never felt inclined to make love with another woman, had always enjoyed a man's touch, despite the few Felly males she'd dated. Some of her species found her too large to be beautiful. Part of her attraction to Terra was simply the woman's exotic appeal—a Terran female, a fighter, and a champ.

Reaching for my Terran half? Amber wondered.

Terra returned with a formall, and Amber began to undress. "No, no, you keep that on," Terra said, shedding her robe and climbing into the formalls.

The sight of her body sent a rush of warmth through Amber.

"Come on, let's get some food before we end up back in the shower. I'll buy."

Amber giggled and followed her into the corridor. The building sounded empty, Amber having found Terra training late at night. She had wandered the sprawling city for most of the day and had somehow found her way back to the arena.

Terra led her down the street past several restaurants, the boulevard here thick with establishments. "No, not that one. I'm so tired of Mongolian. There, that one. How about French?"

Unaccustomed to the various Terran cuisines, Amber said, "Sure."

Sitting across from each other at the table, Amber and Terra tried to puzzle through the foreign-language menu, long-stemmed glasses of water between them, the white tablecloth immaculate.

A Terran waiter not terribly larger than Terra approached, a white kerchief hanging over his shoulder in an oh-so precise way, his bushy black mustache like a caterpillar under his nose, the shnoz a veritable beak protruding from between drawn, disdainful cheeks. He slid to a halt beside their table and kicked the leg. The glasses shook, and a splash of water sloshed from each to splotch the tablecloth.

"How immodest of you ladies to spill—downright gauche. And how dare you appear in our fine establishment of haute cuisine sans haute couture." He didn't prop a hand on his hip, but he might have. "A thirty-percent surcharge will assuage our offended vanity. Oh, but it's you, the Champ," he added, patting Amber delicately on the arm. "For the honor of serving you, the management waives its indignation fee. Now, as to your order, to spare you the embarrassment of having to admit you can't read French, you'll have the fillet of duck—" then he turned and pointed at Terra—"and you'll have the filet mignon. As to the wine, a glass of Chianti, Toulouse '87, will go divine with the arugula and fava-bean crostini, and for dessert, of course, you'll have the wellington pie topped with whipped waterloo cream. Did I get your order right?"

Amber blinked at Terra as the waiter danced away, not waiting for a reply.

"You said you needed my help."

Relieved that the other woman was being so direct, Amber nodded and sighed, biting back her despair. She recounted events from the time she'd been summoned from Felly in the transpod, neglecting to mention the amulet.

"I don't get it. Why you?"

Amber shrugged. "Somehow related to the Emperor's death, but I couldn't say how."

"And this Bati Kochakin, a former Chief of Staff, eh? Now, I don't know politics at all, but isn't that akin to Prime Minister, the one who just took over, this Cyrbodan Occuday?"

Amber nodded. "He said he was being considered for the position. Instead resigned and took to pirating along the outer Perseus Arm. He would have occupied the position Occuday now has."

"You are in a heap o' trouble."

The duck was fabulous and the wine went straight to her head, and Amber found herself telling Terra about the conquest of Felly—not a full conquest but an armistice with a solid containment, complete with an embargo. No one had ever conquered the Felly.

"But this guy did, this Kochakin, eh?" Terra asked. "Contained, conquered, yeah, I understand the difference, but the effect is the same. And then you get bounced off course and land within a klik of his pirate base. I agree, not an accident. But there's something else. How you battled off the Imperials at the pirate base. How you two got to Earth. You don't do those by sharpening your cat claws and getting good at hand-to-hand. No matter. If I were you I wouldn't tell me everything, anyway. You don't unload in the third round unless you have a chance to end it there. You're outmatched by your enemy in size and power, and your only way to victory is to outlast your opponent and hope for a draw. You can't go after him so you gotta let him come after you. You don't know how he'll do that unless you leave yourself open deliberately, draw the punch but watch for the feint. And when he comes for you, analyze his style, pick it apart, expose its weaknesses, exploit the gaps." Terra sighed and pushed aside her plate.

Amber pushed hers aside as well, having found not a bone to pick. She'd emptied the fillet of duck of the scrumptious, delicate meats inside.

"I'm not telling you anything you didn't already know."

Amber nodded. "I just wish I knew where to go, what to do now."

"When you're backed into a corner, make sure it's your own corner." Terra winked at her and called for the check. "We'll have to decline the desert," she told the miffed waiter.

Following her out into the cold, the welterweight's jacket tight around her shoulders, Amber fell into step beside Terra and drew comfort from the woman's arms across her shoulders.

How easy it would be to fold myself into her life and burrow into her sanctuary, Amber thought, having occasionally considered what it would be like to be someone's wife. Become Terra's friend and lover? Amber wondered, knowing Terra would be a good husband.

"Ever hear the saying," Terra asked, " 'Every woman needs a wife'?"

Amber threw her head back and laughed, spinning out of Terra's embrace, embarrassed that her thoughts were so apparent and yet craving the warmth of gentle affiliation that Terra was offering. So easy!

A figure stepped from the alley and cut Terra in half with a blaster.

Without thinking, Amber kicked away the blaster, thrust two knuckles into the larynx, and brought her foot up into the chin. The head snapped back with a pop and the figure crumpled.

"Noooo!" she wailed, cradling Terra's torso to her, the life pouring out of her quickly, blood spilling across Amber, the legs twitching in the gutter nearby.

"Occuday's coming after you, girl," Terra whispered. "Go on, leave me, quick! He'll have back up." And then she died.

Amber fled.

* * *

Kathy looked around before knocking softly on the door.

Professor Tossucan Aigar opened it. His eyes went wide. "Quickly, come in. I'd wondered where you'd gone."

She slipped inside, glanced around.

His home was in stark contrast to his office, the latter as free of personal decoration as the former appeared cluttered.

Esoterica from a variety of cultures bulged threateningly from each surface. A railing headed upstairs had been turned into a 14th century Turkish Man-O-War, a chandelier into an orbital spacepod, a wall-mounted lamp into a cathedral gargoyle. Shelves burst with knickknacks of other ages, a black-lacquered Japanese teapot, a cinnamon-scented Scintillian septometer, an airbrushed-blue Kazakhstani buruka.

"My apologies for the chaos," he said. "My avidity for acquisition far exceeds the size of my house." He wore a dark blue, floor-length robe splashed with a constellation of celestial objects.

Kathy shrugged, happy to see someone she knew. "You wouldn't believe what I've been going through."

"When you disappeared yesterday, I was wondering where to. Seems your father is missing as well. Not a coincidence."

Kathy couldn't keep the worry off her face.

"As I thought. Please, have a seat." He snapped his fingers.

A servant appeared, a gray creature just over three feet tall, its whiskers twizzling skeptically, its small eyes on either side of the conical snout almost ludicrous, and its long gray tail laid out on the floor behind it like the trail of a long evening gown.

"Tea and finger sandwiches for my guest," the professor said.

The gray offworlder scurried away. It looked like one of the ubiquitous Murry, a conquered race that had ingratiated itself to its oppressors by becoming personal slaves to the upper echelons of the Terran hierarchy.

Kathy tried to object. "Look, you don't have to—"

"Simple hospitality," Professor Aigar interrupted, leading her to a chair, its gold veneer claw feet below a winged headrest of elaborate proportion, the headrest wings each resolving into an eagle's head.

The view from between the eagles was disconcerting. I get the impression they'll each dump a glop of bird shit on my shoulders, she thought.

"Tell me what happened."

She recounted everything from the time she'd been confronted by the bloodhound detective at the library door, neglecting to mention the amulet, taking an occasional bite or sip, the professor's eyes remaining on her in quiet contemplation.

"Three times you've alluded to certain events but elided them from your story. By the nature of what you have not said, I know what you have. You're wise not to say what it is or how you used it." The professor rose, stepped to the mantel. He set in motion a device with five balls suspended in a row, each on two strings. "Equal and opposite." His eyes followed the momentum translated through the stationary balls, then he turned toward her.

"His majesty our deceased and beloved Emperor Chingis Khan inveighed upon me to make him a miniature transpod, 'so small I can operate it with my fingers,' he said. Must have been forty years ago, when he was a student of mine. Ambitious, yes, even then. So when he returned ten years later, after having conquered most of the outer Perseus Arm, and asked for three more, of course I balked. 'Look what you did with the first!' He was not pleased that I challenged his having subjugated more than fifty alien civilizations, peaceable peoples who'd in no way harmed him nor intended it. I divagated upon the merits of freedom and the politics of self-determination, while he fulminated about the squandering of resources in fifty races expending their individual efforts toward the same or similar goals, and finally we reached a compromise.

"Why did he compromise, when he might have simply ordered me on pain of death to do his bidding? He was not a man to threaten. No, quite the opposite, which I suspect was his downfall. He nearly didn't contain the Felly, you know. He thought reason and suasion might prevail, but the cat people as you might know are so stubbornly individualistic that he'd have had to persuade each individual Felly.

"The compromise we arrived at was that he would see the conquered races be given a greater voice in Imperial affairs and greater autonomy within their own realms, within reason of course. How he did that was entirely his own affair. I wasn't inclined to involve myself in the frustrating exercise of politics. It flustered me even to argue with him.

"How did I make them? Well of course, using the technology itself. The theory of wave and particle mechanics are both dependent upon the seemingly immutable properties of time, mass, and distance. Once we learned that in addition to being mutable, they were manipulable as well, then that's when the real advancements began. Time as a wave can be condensed to a single point, as we know it was before the universe began. The displacement we now impose in using transpods is mild." He gestured at the five-ball model. "Each displacement has its consequence, and we try to keep these to a minimum. In proportion, the volume kept suspended advances the surrounding universe by the same amount of time in proportion by volume. Hence one person keeping themselves suspended causes an immensurable advance, the proportion of one person to the surrounding universe being infinitesimal. I realize I'm preaching to the choir about fundamentals far more basic than I might entertain when lecturing, but the principle of time as compressible in the universe is important when expanded to the postulate of the multi-verse, the short name for multiple parallel universes.

"When distance is converted to wave and particle principles, it too compensates proportionally. In Newtonian mechanics, an equal and opposite reaction of an apple hitting you on the head is of course your caution the next time you approach the tree.

"Oh, uh, sorry, a little humorous deviation there. Matter has always been held as mutable but only within the strictest guidelines of preservation through change of states. When mass is subject to the mutability of wave mechanics—since mass as a particle was studied ad infinitum, I won't elucidate—we then venture into its compressibility. A black hole couldn't exist without it, of course.

"Here at the confluence of all three we now advance to the interstitial effects of compressing time, distance, and mass. Thus far, when one vector compresses, infinitesimal reactions occur in the surrounding universe. Previous to the advent of the multi-verse into our consciousness, we speculated on nothing further than those infinitesimal effects. But when Transpods operating in close proximity—especially along parallel vectors using similar degrees of compression—some curious deviations began to occur.

"Transpod occupants were being subjected to momentary infusion of all three vectors, in other words, they were being thrown about within the transpods mercilessly, sometimes with fatal effects.

"Yes, I suspect your being subjected to high-vector changes when leaving Canny was caused by precisely the same thing. In other words, someone was trying to interfere with your safe arrival here on Earth.

"How did I make it? Ah, yes, that. I simply reduced the wavelength component of the transpod engine to the size of a pinhead and inserted it into a crystal. The porcelain disc serves to conduct signals to the transpod engine, and the gold ring is simply adornment—a way of attaching the disk to a string or chain or wristband, whatever suits your fancy. How you hold it is what activates its components.

"His Majesty the deceased Emperor liked to wear it around his neck—a highly inconvenient place to have it, in my opinion. Here, I have a glove I'd designed. The amulet goes here, held safely on the back of the hand, hidden under this flap of leather, and by flexing the pinky this way, it brings the disc to the thumb and forefinger. Yes, there, like that.

"Oh dear me, I don't want to see it! Then I'd have to say I knew something that you surely don't want me to disclose." Professor Aigar sat back down and regarded her over his own cup of tea, now long since cold. He sipped in what appeared to be happy oblivion.

Kathy flexed her left pinky a few times to get accustomed to the motion, bemused at the way he could ramble. "So it has time, mass, and distance compressors? All three? What are they?"

Using a one-galacti coin, Professor Aigar demonstrated, holding his left hand in the position as he described them. "Mass," he pinched thumb and forefinger in a circle, the coin encircled. "Time," he pinched the center of the coin between thumb and forefinger, the coin edge visible. "Distance," he held the edge of the coin between thumb and forefinger. "Of course, to prevent its being triggered, it has a corneal reader, a microscopic vidcam with your iris imprinted."

"I have to look at it, you mean."

"Precisely. A small safeguard. You'll notice it glows when you use it. Emitting light to read your iris with."

"Of course. And that's how the Emperor became the Emperor, wasn't it?"

"I'm afraid it was, for better or worse. For a time I supervised the maintenance of his fleet of transpods, a paltry hundred thousand of them. For the trained warrior, such a device made him or her formidable and nearly invincible. People are surprised he had so few, but that too was intended. The fewer there were, the fewer he had to control. His leverage—beside the miniature transpod embedded in the amulet, of course—wasn't in the power he wielded, but in the people he persuaded to do his bidding. He was very persuasive. It was no surprise that his first target and his first conquest was the Canny. You're how old?"

"Thirty," Kathy said. Born just one year after the Canny capitulation, she'd never known freedom, having grown to adulthood entirely under the Terran domination.

But then, I've never endured a Felly attack, either, she thought, the cat people legendary for their stealth and cunning. The perpetual war between Canny and Felly had ceased at the advent of the Terran invasion.

"You've lived all your life under his rule. If nothing else, he enforced peace." The professor sipped tea, his gaze distant.

Kathy wished she had more time, wanting to tap Professor Aigar's vast experience in serving the Emperor Chingis Khan. "I'd like to stay, but the way they came after Mengu, I'm afraid I may be putting you in danger." Kathy shivered, unaccustomed to having to look over her shoulder.

"Are you cold? That formall must be too thin. It gets terribly cold at night here. Where will you go?"

"I don't know." Kathy knew she couldn't return to the abandoned boiler room that she'd shared with Mengu.

"Well, here, at least take this." The professor stood and shrugged out his floor-length robe and handed it to her.

"Oh, I couldn't."

"I insist."

It didn't even reach her ankles, her Canny bulk and height taking up much of the length, but it was roomy enough at shoulders and waist to fit, and did emphasize her bust.

"It'll keep you warm at least. Listen, it's time I take my evening stroll anyway. How about we walk down to the restaurant district, and I'll buy you a Mongolian meal whose memory will make you salivate."

"Maybe not such a good idea." Her droopy jowls tended to drool too much to start with.

"I can see you're hungry."

She'd drooled quite involuntarily.

He donned a plain, padded formall over the thin one he already wore. He excused himself to use the facilities, and invited her to do the same before they left. "Here, I want you to have this." He handed her a small handblaster. "Designed to fit in your palm."

"Very kind of you," she said as they exited his house.

Looking back over her shoulder along the nearly empty street, the handblaster a comfort, the amulet now in its holder on the gloved left hand. While in the restroom, she'd slid it in and had practiced a few times, finding that a few variations in her pinky motion would place the amulet in the three different positions.

The night was bitterly cold, their breath fogging up as it exited their airshells. The professor had also given her fresh batteries and clean filters, the foul Earth air quickly clogging any and all filtration systems within hours. Though pedestrians were sparse, the street seemed as noisy as ever, the ubiquitous vidscreens blathering their inane product pitches to inattentive passersby.

"I can see the question in your face," he said, glancing toward her as they approached a darker stretch. "Why am I helping you?"

Kathy had certainly been wondering.

"The Emperor was a generous man—generous to a fault. He always kept the future of the Empire at heart, and he left little to chance. Even his untimely death was surely an event he'd planned for. Space knows there are enough Brutuses for our Caesars. I suspect that you're as much a part of his—"

A figure leaped out and blasted the Professor.

Kathy flexed her left pinky and pinched the crystal between thumb and forefinger.

The world froze beyond a fuscous curtain.

The blast had already cleaved the Professor through the spine.

She howled mournfully, silent in timelessness, wished she might reverse time, wished she'd refused to wear his robe, wished she'd not come to seek his help at all.

A cold murderous rage replaced her sorrow and guilt. The assassin had tried to kill her, had instead killed the innocent Professor.

Kathy removed the blaster from the assassin's hand and hurled it into the night; it froze beyond her timeless umbrella. Using the handblaster given to her by the Professor, she then sliced through each of the assassin's legs at the knee and each arm at the elbow, then burned out the eyes from the sockets. Revenge, although a dish best served cold, was tasteless without the victim's knowing it. This assassin would live out his life without limb or sight, and would only have his foul murder of the Professor to regret.

Kathy went through his pockets, emptied them into hers. The sensation of motion amidst motionlessness was akin to being on an alien planet, the utter silence disconcerting.

She turned and put as much distance behind her as she could, and when she couldn't run anymore, her tongue lolling from the side of her mouth, she released her hold on the amulet.

The surrounding world slammed her with noise, and she realized she was whimpering pitiably. She found a recessed doorway, and ignoring the rank smell of marinated urine, she curled up inside and wept disconsolately.

* * *

Theresa sighed and rolled off him, and he nuzzled her breast, the pull at the nipple echoed in a pull on her organs.

She'd somehow found her way back to the racetrack, the chaotic city overwhelming, the strange faces and odd smells disconcerting.

Wandering anonymously held a certain appeal. On Equy, where other races were non-existent, Terrans were scarce, and full-blooded specimens of her race were ubiquitous, Theresa had stood out like a spot of green mold on a chunk of orange cheese. On Earth, the mold was multicolored and multilayered, so thick the cheese couldn't be found, and Teresa went unnoticed. The appeal of anonymity had lost its moldy luster in the first hour in the dark, dirty city.

When she'd returned to the racetrack, the first thing she'd asked for had been a shower. Dripping wet, she'd gone to find him, and then exhausted, she'd slept.

He'd awakened her just as dawn tinted the windows, and they'd made love again, Jimmy as generous as the steeds he rode, this time Theresa riding him.

"I need to go," she said, not wanting him to get reprimanded, the on-grounds quarters unlikely to tolerate guests.

"Uh, well, I've been looking for a stablehand." Jimmy's face turned red, looking embarrassed to be asking. "Ever work with horses before?"

Theresa almost laughed, the Equy similar to the ancient Terran species. I really need the place to stay, she was thinking, and Jimmy's very nice. "If I work here, then I shouldn't stay here with you."

Jimmy nodded. "There's a bunk at the other end with a hot plate and shower stall. And you'd be pitching horse dung all day, which I can't get anyone to do for any price."

"How much?" Theresa asked.

They negotiated a price, and she grinned. She didn't mention she'd been pitching Terran dung all day. "When do I start?"

Jimmy showed her the lodgings, a stall too small for a horse. But it was warm, private, and hers. Jimmy got her a set of formalls like his, green and white checks, and showed her what to do. By noon, she smelled like a horse of course, her boots caked to the ankle. I guess I'm supposed to shovel shit for a living, she thought, bemused.

That afternoon, as the pale disc they called "the Sun" neared the western horizon, its reflection visible only on the surrounding towers, Theresa was hauling a bucket of water to old Emperor, the stud roan male who'd pleased her on her first night at the racetrack, when sharp voices outside the stable interrupted their flirtations.

"I swear, Ma'am! I don't know what got into him! He's never failed to stud for us!"

Theresa peered out into the corral.

Clad in full riding gear, his colors blazing, Jimmy was cowering under the baleful glare of the pointy-titted woman in the simple sere uniform, her hair pulled back so tight it gave her an instant face lift, a Terran hand etched on the metal armband, palm out.

"Who's that?!" She'd spied Theresa instantly.

"Uh, Tracy, my new stablehand. You said I could hire one." He sounded afraid that she would countermand his decision.

"Oh? Oh, I did, of course. Step out and show yourself, girl. Fine stocky build you've got. Come here, don't be shy."

Theresa stepped toward the pair. Beyond them, the stadium was coming to life, the towers of klieg lights difficult to look at.

"Look at those bones. Strong as a horse is my guess." She turned to Jimmy, standing beside her one of the ubiquitous Murry, quiet as a mouse. "Fine choice, looks like. Built for the job, certainly."

Theresa stood a full head taller than the other woman, but the size of her breasts got Theresa to wondering whether she might have had them augmented. They certainly commanded attention. "Pleased," Theresa said, extending a hand. Abruptly, she wiped it on her formalls, then extended it again.

"Already been at work I see."

Her hand remained empty. "Yes, ma'am," Theresa said, lowering it. "Sorry, guess it's a bit dirty." She looks like she detests walking on dirt because she might get dirty! Theresa thought, keeping the thought carefully off her face.

"Always glad to see people hard at work. Know anything about horses, such as why Emperor went flaccid when we tried to stud him out yesterday?"

"Commander Tureg, I, uh, don't think—"

"He was constipated, commander," Theresa interrupted. "I shoveled out a clump twice the usual size."

"Oh, uh, I see. Didn't know that could be an issue. All right. Guess we'll have to watch for that next time."

"I started a notebook to track his movements, Commander. And he really should have his urine measured as well, checked for infection and ketones."

The iron-haired woman's eyes narrowed. "Ketones?"

"If he's spilling ketones into his urine, it means he needs a work up for diabetes, maybe hypertension."

"Well, see too it, Jimmy. This girl's a find. Wouldn't have thought of that myself. Are you bringing her to Belmont when we race Emperor two weeks from now? Hope so, seems to know what she's doing." Commander Tureg nodded at Theresa. "Carry on, miss."

Dismissed, Theresa retreated to the barn while Jimmy stayed behind to chat a bit more.

What a royal witch! she thought, snorting in disgust. She brought the horses their evening hay, this bale more moist than the dry, crappy straw they usually gave.

"This moist enough for you, Emperor?"

"Sure is, Beautiful," he replied, his Equy heavily-accented but needing no translation even so.

Theresa patted him contentedly while he fed.

Jimmy stopped outside the stall. "You gonna watch the races?"

"Can I? I've never seen a horserace."

From the corral, Jimmy pointed across the track, the Emperor's booth clearly festooned with banners and streamers, backed by thick, blood-red curtains. "If you peek from behind the curtains, you can see the whole track without anyone knowing you're there. No one's used the box since the Emperor's death."

The Emperor's horses, she discovered, were the only ones to have their own stable, the two other stables at the track having to be shared amongst various nobles. Emperor, the Emperor's prize stallion, wouldn't be racing tonight, needing to rest up for the Belmont stakes two weeks hence. As she wandered around the track, amazed at the sight of the elaborately-dressed and -coiffed upper crust of Imperial society, Theresa wondered that they didn't have anything better to do than sit around and watch a bunch of small men hump huge horses around a track. Don't they have an Empire to run? She snuck up to the Emperor's box just to see what Jimmy had been talking about.

Peeking out from between the plush curtains behind the Emperor's booth, Theresa watched the first race with some excitement, finding herself getting caught up in the exhilaration.

The booth to one side, was that of the Prime Minister, Cyrbodan Occuday. Theresa saw Commander Tureg sitting beside him.

During the quieter moments between races, she could overhear snatches of their conversation.

"... haven't found out a thing about those three, have you, Sorkha? Have you?" Prime Minister Occuday's voice was almost accusatory. "They'll say Commander Sorkha Tureg has lost her edge, needs to resign as Chief of Military Intelligence, can't do even the simplest thing like find three half-breed females in Ulaanbaatar!"

"Patience, Sire, and bite your tongue. We both know there's not another mind sharper than mine. I'll bring them to you, I assure you. One is already being monitored, and the other two will soon be under surveillance. An unfortunate circumstance, the deaths of that professor and boxer; I put them under guard, fearing for their lives from just such sources, but those two half-breeds killed one guard and maimed the other."

"That was them? How do you know?"

"Convincing evidence at both crime scenes, Sire. And as I thought, these three expatriates—Chingis's associates, heretofore-useless bags of hot wind, expostulating on your honor's expropriation of our Sovereign's minority. Forgive me. Sire, for expounding again on the topic, but as soon as they're dead, I'll sleep much better."

"Hold your friends close, Sorkha, but hold your enemies closer. Just as you should be holding these half-breeds."

"You wouldn't believe, Sire, how close the one is held. Nearly within arm's reach. Where I'll soon have the other—"

A roar went up, horses launching from the starting gate.

Chapter 10

Amber walked up the street, emergency hovers converging on the gun store, their blaring sirens muted through the shield. She kept her thumb and forefinger securely around the amulet until the store was far behind her, knowing they'd be searching for her.

Her difficulty was obscuring her face. Although the Felly population on Earth was somewhere in the hundreds of thousands, her Felly looks instantly identified her as an object of suspicion.

The few times she'd been spotted, she'd slipped away using the amulet. Now, as a matter of course, she used the amulet to obscure herself every few minutes, on two occasions surprising a nearby surveiller, who'd then panicked and alerted the chain of command that she'd disappeared. They had tried to kill her a month ago, and nothing indicated they weren't still trying.

Their mistake had been not succeeding the first time.

She'd seen the new stories, her face broadcast across the Empire. A suspected Felly rebel had assassinated the welterweight women's champion and her bodyguard outside of the restaurant where the champion had dined, the motive unknown. Press speculation described it as the result of the Champion's rebuff of the rebel's request for assistance in the Felly cause. Because of the misinformation, she was now a target for zealots.

The Felly government was denying involvement—and denying that any such organized rebellion existed, a point they proved simply by citing the perennial Felly disorganization—pointing to the intergalactic missile strike on the Felly homeworld as another act of insurgency protesting the government's continued cooperation with the Terran conquerors.

For the past month, since nearly being killed outside the restaurant, Amber had been conducting heists like this: Walking into armament stores using the amulet, grabbing as much as she could carry of high-caliber weapons and ammunition, and walking out again. The dozen places she'd robbed were in no particular order or geographic location, without a pattern to predict where she might go next.

Entering the abandoned warehouse where she'd squatted a month ago, Amber walked to the sixth-floor landing to the windowless room in the center, whose door was welded shut against intruders. There she unloaded her take.

Rifles, handguns, and ammunition clattered onto a pile on the floor.

Divested of her satchel of weapons, Amber activated the matter translator, encircling the amulet with thumb to forefinger. Stepping through the door, she looked around, and then walked the perimeter. Seeing nothing amiss, nearly the entire floor visible except for the windowless office in the center, Amber then made a circuit, peering out each window, looking for surveillance, always on the prowl.

Returning to the room, she sorted through her acquisitions, categorizing them by size and strength, matching the ammunition with their respective firearms. When finished, she looked around her arsenal.

Against each wall was a set of weapons any mercenary would be proud of. Four sets of weapons, each laid out for quick arming, each containing handhelds, shoulder mounts, ammo belts, back launchers, hip holsters, armor plates, helmets, and goggles.

Amber had practiced with each weapon in the dead of night at the local firing range, experimenting with the transpod amulet at the same time.

Looking around her arsenal, which she had set up for quick access, she reviewed her plan, the most difficult part of her preparation still ahead: how to find out who was trying to kill her.

Amber knew no matter what she did, the attempt on her life would always be misconstrued by the government and the media as her having assassinated the champion, not some government operative's trying to assassinate her.

She wasn't sure which infuriated her more—their trying to kill her, or their pinning the blame on her.

Terra deserves better than that, Amber thought, remembering what the Champ had told her: "It's clear you can drop 'em in record time." What Terra had taught her was how to look at the long picture.

Which was still a cloudy murk.

* * *

Kathy poked her head into the vault, and then stepped inside, the penumbra of her transpod making the solid armor walls as thin as air.

Transactions rarely handled with cash anymore, galacti bills now sat mainly in vaults like this, their electronic ownership changing hands thousands of times daily, all the while the bills sat here, untouched, unsullied, and safe. For the past month, since nearly being killed outside the professor's house, Kathy had been conducting heists like this: Walk carefully into a bank vault using the amulet, grab a handful of high-denomination bills, and walk out again. The dozen banks she'd robbed were in no particular order or geographic location, without a pattern to predict where she might go next.

Nicking five bundles of thousand-galacti bills in a flicker of the amulet, Kathy thought, I'll finally have enough to do what I want.

The vault sensors tripped, lights flashed, bells rang, and steel bars slammed into place, all of which happened through a thick veil, muted and dimmed by the amulet's effects. Once she'd become comfortable that no one could see, feel, touch, or hear her, she'd enjoyed sitting back and watching the panicked bank staff, police investigators, and emergency responders hustle helplessly about, each desperately wanting to look as though they were doing something.

But not this time.

This her last heist, Kathy calculated that she had enough cash to do what she wanted, and didn't stay to watch the confusion that followed. She made her way carefully out of the bank, always leery of her footing, the one place not completely protected by the amulet. A hard knot inside her, Kathy strode toward central Ulaanbaatar, the stack of bills in one hand, the amulet in the other, toward an abandoned warehouse that she'd squatted in a month ago.

On the fifth floor of the warehouse, Kathy reached the landing, and glanced down the stairwell to make sure she wasn't being followed. She hadn't mastered the space translation controls of the amulet well enough to put herself precisely where she needed. Within a few kilometers was as accurate as she'd gotten. The stairwell was silent, nothing moving above or below. Occasionally she'd heard movement from the sixth and topmost floor of the warehouse above her, but she attributed it to rats.

Encircling the amulet, she stepped through the wall. Street-level light streaked the ceiling, hovercars whining past.

Her Canny face distinct, she knew she was easy to spot, and ever since the murder of Professor Aigar, which had been pinned on her, she was a hunted woman. She was infuriated that his murder had been blamed on her, the speculation being that she'd asked him to assist the Canny in rebelling against their Terran overlords. Rebellion a rare characteristic in a Canny, the Government's denial of any involvement was taken at face value, despite its inability to explain the interstellar missile strike on the Canny homeworld some four months ago.

In the month since the attempt on her life, they had not tried again, but she had moved with such stealth that she doubted they'd had the opportunity. Leaving herself vulnerable to attack, she reasoned, would only expose the proxies carrying out the assassination order, not the person or organization issuing the order.

She sighed, not sure still how to approach the problem.

Allies, she thought, I have to have allies.

Kathy then walked to the windowless room in the center, whose door was locked with a simple palm sensor. Without electricity, it remained locked.

Kathy stepped through the wall, and only then loosened her grip on the amulet. She turned on a battery lamp, unshouldered her pack and dumped its contents on the floor. She instantly regretted the noise, holding herself still and silent for five minutes afterward. Paranoid that someone had heard, she used the amulet to make a quick circuit of the entire floor again, surveilling the street from each window as she went. The area around the warehouse appeared to be clear.

A thump from the floor above startled her.

I thought this warehouse was abandoned, she thought, the reason I chose it to start with.

Her first week here, she had waited on the fifth floor in silence for the least sign of occupancy, leaving only for meals. Even in the vermin appeared to have abandoned it. Then she had searched all the other floors, finding some minimal signs of recent activity on the sixth floor but nothing else on the first four floors. She'd dismissed the stirred dust on the sixth floor and then had begun to build her treasury.

The thump she'd just heard was the first sign she might not be alone. Kathy pinched the amulet crystal between thumb and forefinger to stop time, then encircled it with her other hand. Suspended in time in an alternate universe, Kathy headed for the stairs.

At the sixth floor landing, she inspected the multiple locks on the door. None looked jimmied, and all appeared secure. Inside the flat, which like the fifth floor was open space with a single locked room in the center, all looked similar.

Kathy sensed something was different.

The feel.

Determined to find the difference, she strode around the perimeter, much as she had the fifth floor upon her return.

She'd almost completed the circuit when—

She struck something.

Bouncing off it, she almost lost her hold on the amulet, which felt warmer than usual, its crystal glowing brighter.

Nothing visible. Bewildered, she probed the place, finding a solid obstruction, but not able to see what it was.

Think! she told herself, If I'm in a parallel universe with time stopped, what possible obstruction could I encounter? And what would cause the amulet to overheat?

Rather than risk the amulet's burning out or at least causing her fingers to blister, Kathy backed away and inspected the remainder of the flat. Nothing unusual except the slight indication of a trail though the inch-thick dust, which she'd noticed a week after occupying the fifth floor. On closer inspection, the trail—absent actual footprints—appeared to make a circuit around the perimeter.

Which I was following! she thought.

Consciously or not, she'd followed the trail. Then she realized why: like her circuit of the fifth floor perimeter, the trail followed the path that gave an occupant the best view of the street below.

Someone must be surveilling the surrounding area from this floor, just as I'm doing on the fifth!

She looked toward the center office, the windowless room that stood in the center of the building, the sixth floor identical in layout to the floor she occupied below.

Kathy stuck her head through the wall.

Guns of various calibers were stacked against the walls, ammunition piled beside each, backpacks and shoulder harnesses and armor arranged carefully in sets. Enough firepower to launch an assault on a fortress.

Like that at Kharkhorin, the Imperial Intelligence Headquarters. Where the Empire kept its prized prisoners, where brutal interrogations were conducted, where people disappeared, never to be seen again. Where they'd taken Mengu Larine, former Commander and leader of the assault on the Canny homeworld, Canis Majoris III.

Kathy pulled her head back through the wall and glanced down at the amulet in her hand, wondering who else possessed one and how it had been obtained.

And why.

* * *

Theresa shrugged at Jimmy. "Look, I know it's odd, and I know you feel left out, but I have to take these opportunities. I mean, I'd be stupid not to, and she'd probably fire me if I refused." Theresa had just been promoted to lead talent scout for the Imperial Equestrian Division, a position supervised directly by Commander Sorkha Tureg. It was the third such promotion since she'd joined the stables one month ago.

"You don't horse around, do you?" Jimmy said.

Of course Jimmy feels jealous, Theresa told herself, pleading with him to see reason. What she didn't tell Jimmy was that

Commander Tureg had appointed Theresa to the position only as a means of covering Theresa's real activity.

"You're an astute observer of people," she'd told Theresa, getting up from the divan in her office, pulling herself from the embrace of the most voluptuous female Theresa had ever seen.

If the bovine were chewing on something, she'd just be a cow, Theresa thought.

"Leave us, my pea," Sorkha had told the woman, and then she'd swung her double barrels at Theresa. "I see the way you watch Jimmy, the scorn in your eyes at his ineptitude. I need your powers of observation for an entirely different purpose, a clandestine purpose. You'll tell Jimmy that you've been assigned scouting duties for his majesty's Equestrian Division, a task I would never assign to anyone else, of course, but he doesn't need to know that. I'll provide you with a list of potential acquisitions that you'll memorize, but your real task will be finding these two offworlders." And she'd shoved two dossiers at Theresa.

Theresa had spent several hours perusing the two dossiers, which commander Tureg wouldn't let out of her sight. She'd had to endure the slurping and sloshing from the nearby couch, the Commander's cries of pleasure so sharp that Theresa wanted to duck and hide under the desk lest the paroxysms accidentally cause the double barrels to fire.

When she'd returned to the stables, she'd leapt onto Jimmy's single barrel cannon before telling him she'd been promoted yet again.

Theresa watched him slink sullenly away and felt relieved, not wanting further strife, knowing she had even worse news from him. The promotion included a suite of rooms inside the palace, and three personal servants chosen by Commander Tureg herself.

The suite of rooms was near the back of the palace, and just a floor up from the guards' quarters, but Teresa loved it instantly, the walls adorned with paintings from ancient Mongolian history, prominent among the depictions the Emperor Genghis Khan.

In one, a blistering sandstorm buffeted the young Temujin astride a horse, the tip of his knife blooded, and a cut vein on the horse's shoulder squirting fresh blood into Temujin's mouth.

With but a single glance at her new quarters, Theresa decided that she'd never return to live in the stables again.

Stepping into the open curtainless shower, Theresa made her new servants scrub her rough hide three times. "I want you to scrub that stable stench right off me."

To her delight, she discovered a wardrobe of fancy silks, patterned and styled after the dress of the ancient Jin Dynasty, which the Emperor Genghis Khan had overthrown. Like most conquerors of China, the conquerors had adopted so many customs of the subjugated peoples that they looked and sounded like them, leaving historians with the proverbial question, "Who conquered whom?"

Luxuriating in her new robes atop a cush couch, Theresa pulled out the two stills that Commander Tureg had allowed her to take from the dossiers, one of each offworlder.

The Felly, Amber Calico, a renowned fighter, sprouted whiskers from a button nose, but the scorn in the eyes cancelled any inclination to call her cute.

The Canny, Kathy Mongrel, her droopy ears, eyes, and cheeks masking the calculator brain underneath, had the moist snout like all her ilk.

Both had arrived on Terra some four months before, the dossiers had said, to begin infiltrating the Imperial power structure and unseat the heir Kublai Khan to free their respective homeworlds from the Terran dominion.

"Why don't they join forces?" Theresa had asked Sorkha.

"Precisely our fear. Their assassinating that professor and that boxing champion on the same day indicates they might already be conspiring."

"Why the boxer? I know it's says the Felly likely approached her for help, but even that seems farfetched."

"Who knows?" Sorkha had said. "The Prime Minister is equally concerned. Another of the many questions that I hope you'll answer. Now, here are the 'acquisitions' that you'll be 'scouting' for in the next two weeks. You must find these two rebellious offworlders quickly. Get to it!"

Theresa fingered the amulet in the pocket of her formalls, wondering whether she should use it.

I'd better not, she thought, still mystified that they'd taken Chabi prisoner. Theresa's delicate inquiries had been met with stone-cold bewilderment. Some had heard the name from years before, but no one could recall anything recent, nor say where she might be now.

And what about me? Theresa wondered. Why was I brought to Earth?

Chapter 11

Clad in weaponry weighing as much as she did, Amber slipped into the compound at Kharkhorin, the Imperial Intelligence Headquarters, where the Empire kept its high-value detainees.

Somewhere here, they've got Bati, she thought, the amulet clutched in the circle of thumb and forefinger. Her surroundings were dimmed as though behind tinted glass.

Amber knew she'd have to be armed to extract Bati from the Kharkhorin Fortress.

Three layers of buzzing electric fence perimetered the compound, each layer crowned with thorny wire. The outermost battlement was honeycombed with patrol routes, foot soldiers leading large dogs on patrol.

Uncanny, how similar they were to the Canny.

Motion detectors, chemical sniffers, infrared beams, directional microphones, and armed drones prowled the next two inner battlements, each reaching twenty meters into the sky. A ribbed dome capped with turrets kept at bay any airborne intruders, the turrets bristling with guns, and red-lighted beacons blared warnings across radio frequencies for air traffic to reroute or be blasted from the sky.

Sliding through these security measures like water through a sieve, Amber worked her way toward the detainee complex five floors underground, following mostly the established route.

In practicing with the amulet, she'd nearly fallen several stories when she'd inadvertently walked through walls into elevators shafts. The convoluted passageways leading ever downward into the Fortress were riddled with checkpoints, the bored and yawning guards not able to see her, the quiescent sensors unable to sense her.

I wonder what kind of shape he's in, Amber thought, trying to puzzle through the signs on the walls, Mongolian just looking like random symbols. Buryat, the traditional Mongolian script, was widely used throughout the Empire, but because the Felly had been contained in their natal star system for the last twenty-five years, the language had never been imposed upon them, unlike elsewhere, most local languages having made room for the foreign tongue of the Terran overlord.

Fortunately, Amber had obtained a sketch of the compound from Betty, the sketch artist. Where the old woman had obtained a map of intelligence headquarters, Amber didn't know, but as she descended deeper into the bowels, she realized how accurate it was.

They must have brought Betty down here, Amber thought, wondering if they'd tortured the old woman.

Amber descended a last stairwell, the amulet's penumbra dulling the glare off the plain white walls and the glint off the weapons held by the guards.

Five checkpoints along this corridor alone, Amber knew, having memorized the map, not daring to bring it with her and risk exposing Betty's role in helping her.

Unlike the guards at the numerous checkpoints above, these guards looked attentive, their eyes quartering every bit of the plain, stark corridor.

"What do you suppose that old bitch Tureg wants us to look out for?" one muttered to the other.

"Hush or she'll hear you," the other hissed back, not taking her eyes off the corridor.

"That old bitch'd give me promotion for calling her that. Besides, she reads minds anyway. When she was looking at me, I just knew she was listening to my thoughts."

The female guard snorted. "As though you'd ever have a thought worth listening to. She's got far more important skulls to crack than yours or mine."

"Yeah? Well then how'd she know I would've liked to fondle those double barrel cannons she's got? When she was younger, that is."

"Younger, hell," the female said, "I thought you'd put your gun in your pocket."

Amber slid past them through the foot-thick door. These guards also looked tenaciously alert, as though warned. She wondered who the "bitch Tureg" was, and how she'd suspected that Amber might attempt an extraction.

Unless the others had been detained as well.

The sketches Betty had shown her of the three former commanders who'd served Chingis Khan and the three half-breed women—among them Amber—reminded her that perhaps she wasn't alone.

Alone in what?

Always the question, Amber thought, walking through the next armored door toward the third checkpoint.

These guards too looked unnaturally alert.

She slipped between them.

At the fourth checkpoint were four guards, one pair coming on shift, one pair going off. Amber wondered at the lengths of their shifts, knowing a savvy commander would limit them, the human brain rarely able to maintain long hours of hypervigilance.

Or Felly brain, for that matter, Amber thought, opponent physiology the subject of long study by Felly neurologists.

Know your enemy well, Amber's instructors had taught her, and know yourself better.

Beyond the fourth checkpoint, the corridor suddenly turned into an examination chamber, every conceivable device focused on her. Beyond the veil cast by the amulet, Amber noted now this pair of guards stood stone-faced, weapons aimed, and fingers on triggers.

All these deterrents, Amber was thinking. She wondered what other high-value detainees were being kept buried five levels underground, what kind of information the Empire would never let see the light of day.

Beyond the last checkpoint was a stairwell, a pair of guards every five steps. The cavern that it descended into looked like a zoo. Rows of cages marched away in each direction, a hundred total she counted, all visible from above, their tops open. Catwalks lined the cavern, guards strolling both directions along them, the ceiling crisscrossed with catwalks. Forty guards in all just on the catwalks.

Amber immediately saw the difficulty.

Once she contacted Bati and brought him under the amulet's penumbra, the guards peering down from above would almost certainly notice his absence.

Were the other four people whose sketches Betty showed me also being detained here? she wondered, knowing she wouldn't be able to extract but one.

Somewhere, between the sounds of boots on metal grate, she heard a drip.

Plunk, plunk, plunk.

Despite the popularity of Chinese water torture in common lore, Amber doubted the drip was intended, sealing a cavern this size from underground seepage impossible. These Mongols didn't strike her as smart enough to use it as torture.

The dripping gave her an idea.

She descended the stairs and walked up and down the rows of cells, each row separated by fixed blinds—slats turned at angles to prevent prisoners from making visible contact with each other. Amber also noted sonic baffles suspended above each cell, sound emitters that chirped occasionally, their purpose to prevent the detainees from communicating with each other through sound, by talking, tapping walls or pipes, clapping, or any other means.

Inside each cell, Amber noted, where the basic amenities: a cot fixed to the floor, a waste hole for excrement, a water source and shallow basin for washing, and a slot in the cage door for meal trays. She entered an unoccupied cell—the only one she could find—and examined the spigot closely. A mere nub with a hole in the center, beside it a motion sensor, the basin set low below it, not large enough or high enough for a person to crawl under, sitting fifteen centimeters above the floor—high enough to wash a person's private parts, but only in extreme discomfort.

The cell was two meters by two meters, just large enough for a person to stretch out, but not large enough to pace. Solid walls separated each cell in a pod, with two sides having open bars, and four cells in each quat, the plumbing routed to the center of each quad, each quad separated from others by the baffle slats.

In that layout, Amber concluded that prisoners in adjacent cells might communicate by tapping, but that they could only do so with other detainees in that quad pod. Since each quad stood alone, without adjacent walls to other quads, communicating between quads was impossible.

Walking through the cavern, Amber located Bati and the other two former commanders who'd served the deceased Emperor. The other two offworlders whom Betty had sketched, the Canny and the Equy, didn't appear to be among the prisoners.

Looking at Bati though the bars, Amber was struck by how much he'd aged, his cheeks sagging, his prison formalls rumpled, his face furred with gray stubble.

She checked in on the other two, looking at each one carefully to fix their faces in her mind. She still wasn't sure she was going to free them, as much as she hated seeing anyone imprisoned.

Getting Bati out was her priority, and she really wasn't sure how she was going to do that.

Bati's cell was one of the farthest from the exit, the cavern having only the one egress. The quad beside it was equally far, the two rows of quads six deep. Any diversion would have to be in the middle of the path that they'd have to traverse.

I wish there were a better way, she thought.

The amulet in her hand was warm, she noticed.

This is what it did the other night!

Unlike the other night, the amulet stayed warm. In addition, in the white mother-of-pearl disk where the crystal lay embedded, was a glowing orange point. The crystal itself glowed bright orange as well, bright enough that it hurt her eyes to look at it. The off-center orange point moved closer to the crystal, both of them brightening, the crystal growing warmer.

Then the orange point blinked off then on.

The overhead pipes burst apart.

"Now!" a hoarse voice whispered.

Surprised, dismayed, Amber leaped into Bati's cell.

* * *

Kathy examined the pipes ribbing the ceiling and knew what to do.

She pinched the crystal, stopping time, then set about dismantling each cage, all forty-eight of them. She worked slowly but methodically, taking care where to aim her laser, not wanting to hurt the detainees accidentally. Each cell needed only six joists cut through for its two barred walls to fall. Suspended in time, they would only fall when Kathy unpinched the crystal.

Once finished with the cages, she turned her attention to the overhead piping. With the precision of a fluid dynamics engineer, she perforated the pressurized water pipes with her laser where the pipes sank from the ceiling into each quad-cage cellblock.

Once finished, Kathy returned to the cellblock where Mengu was being held and homed in on the other.

Earlier that day, as she'd been sorting the cash she'd robbed from another bank, Kathy had been alerted by the warming amulet of an amulet-using person nearby. Quickly, she'd masked herself and located the source: the sixth floor of the abandoned warehouse.

Following the person, whom she couldn't see, Kathy had found herself crossing the city and perpetrating the highly-feared fortress of Kharkhorin, where Bati was imprisoned. Wondering if the person were armed from the arsenal she'd found on the sixth floor, Kathy suspected that the person, who still remained invisible to her, was there to create mayhem.

When the person stopped beside the cell curtaining Mengu, Kathy knew she'd guessed right.

After discovering the cache of weapons, Kathy had toyed with the idea of setting up cameras on the floor above hers, and perhaps getting a visual of this other amulet wielder. Already she'd suspected it was the other "rebel" who'd "assassinated" the welterweight champion Terra McFall, a Felly named Amber, the two assassination reports too coincidental.

Her having been called a rebel had infuriated her. I'm no more rebel than the heir Kublai Khan! she'd thought at the time.

Inspecting her work while frozen in timelessness, she sighed. How do I signal the other person? she wondered, frowning at the forlorn-looking figure of Mengu in the next cell.

I'll just start time, whisper, "Now!" and stop it again.

Kathy started time, the overhead pipes bursting, klaxons blaring, and then she whispered, "Now!" at the shapeless shape beside her. Then she pinched the stone and slammed the brakes on time.

Stepping to Mengu's side, she smiled.

He was half-standing, coming out of his sitting position on a low bunk, eyes toward the ceiling, water already sprinkled on his brow.

She started time and released the amulet, took his arm and gripped it again.

The surprise in his eyes was replaced with a smile. "I knew you'd come to get me. Very pleasant to see you, Kathy. Now, if you've a moment or two, my good friends in the next cell would certainly like to come with us."

"Friends? You've got friends down here? Among these thieves and reprobates? Listen, Mengu, I followed somebody down here." And she told him why she thought the other person also had an amulet.

Mengu nodded. "And you think that person has come for a similar reason? Well, what do you suppose we do? You're the one with the amulet."

She told him, figuring that they could watch from the safety of a parallel universe, and at least see if either of the other two prisoners disappeared from his or her cell.

Mengu safely inside the shell of the amulet, Kathy walked with him into the next cell and immediately hit the other person's shell; in spite of their occupying space in another universe, their interstitial field could not interfere with another interstitial field, the harmonics inter-resonating and repelling with each other.

Kathy pulled him around to the other man's side. "What's his name?"

"Bati Kochakin, conqueror of the Felly—well, no one really conquered them—and former Chief of Staff to his Imperial Highness, Chingis Khan."

"You said you had two friends. Where's the other?"

Mengu gestured her to follow into the third cell of the four-cell block.

A gray-haired woman stared stonily at the ceiling, her small frame looking frail. On her face was a grin.

"Chabi Schahahaday, former two-star General, Commander of the third and sixth division of his Highness's navy, and conqueror of the Equy."

Kathy frowned. "What do you suppose she's doing here?"

"Happened across a young Equy whose transpod malfunctioned."

Kathy gasped, "Like mine?"

Mengu nodded. "And guess what Bati was doing here?"

"What? The same?" Kathy was puzzled. "And you three were able to discuss all this over lunch, I suppose?"

"We devised a method of talking that didn't involve using our voices; instead we tapped on the walls that separated us. If we'd tried to talk, those things—" he pointed to the sonic emitter hanging from the ceiling over the cell—"would have emitted wave-cancellation sound. But our tapping was limited. All I know is that the Felly's name is Amber, the Equy's name is Theresa, and all three of you appeared about the same time—right after the Emperor's death, and that all you have in common is possession of an amulet, and your transpods appear to have gone awry, taking each of you to the one person most likely to help you."

"And as you've said before, nothing happens in Chingis Khan's Empire that he didn't plan or prepare for."

"Precisely. Not much chance to discuss that with my colleagues, given the limitations of our communicator system."

"You said 'appear to have gone awry.' Are you thinking that it wasn't accidental?"

Mengu frowned. "I'm afraid not. In the process of getting transferred here, I encountered a few acquaintances—"

"More thieves and reprobates?"

"—who tell me that three intergalactic missile strikes demolished a substantial area of each Capitol. Targeted strikes on the

Felly, Canny, and Equy homeworlds. All at the moment of, or shortly after, the Emperor's death. We should try to find the list of dead or missing to see if you recognize any names."

"You think the explosions blew us off course? Caused the transpods to malfunction?"

"Perhaps." Mengu smiled mirthlessly. "But let's get to this business of freeing our friends. We haven't got all day."

"Actually," Kathy retorted, "we've got the rest of time."

* * *

Theresa looked both ways from the dark alley where she'd been lurking, the empty warehouse across the street from her. The occasional hover hissed past, too few to be a real concern. Passersby were so rare in this virtually abandoned rustbelt that Theresa had no fear of being seen—except by them.

They'd been easy to trace.

Criminals are so stupid, she was thinking, scanning the six-floor building from top to bottom again. A small blurb on the billboard news two days ago had piqued her interest, the reporter mentioning three seemingly unrelated robberies of banks in Ulaanbaatar, the sums too small to merit blazing twelve-foot headlines or preview-blaring announcements, but the similarity of the robberies had finally caught some metro-desk editor's attention.

With her employ as Commander Tureg's clandestine sleuth had come access to crime report databases—the non-publications available only to investigative agencies. Instantly, Theresa had spotted a pattern—a circular area where the robberies had occurred. The police detective working the robberies had grumbled about "Imperial interference," but had divulged the information he'd gathered. He'd checked the doors and locks on all the abandoned buildings and other empty rotting hulks in the area, including the warehouse, but had found no evidence of entry, forced or otherwise.

A heat scan and an electricity use survey had instantly pinpointed the warehouse, and Theresa had staked it out since morning.

Then, an hour ago, the heat sensor had detected a slight increase at the southwest loading dock, where a bank of roll-up doors sat bolted shut. The heat increase to the concrete walkway was so slight that Theresa had almost dismissed it. Then she'd turned the scanner to the street where that walkway led, and outlined on the asphalt were two sets of footprints, like moons through a thin cloud layer.

But I didn't see anyone leave the building! she'd thought at the time, bewildered that the tracks appeared without anyone's making them.

Not wanting to expose herself by trying to follow the invisible pair, Theresa traced the steps backward to the west-most of the south doors, and then she'd waited, continuing to scan the concrete trying to detect their return.

When an hour had gone past without anyone's return, Theresa decided to investigate the building. Thumb and forefinger encircling the amulet, she stepped through the locked door, inspecting the locks.

Then she noticed that the door had been welded shut.

What else could they be using but an amulet?

She dropped her gaze to her own, realizing that the dossiers on the Felly and Canny had said nothing about their having possession of such a device. Now, the bank robberies made sense! The detective had blathered on and on about the difficulty of subverting either the security controls or the fiscal controls, and he hadn't really been sure whether the thefts were outright robberies or very sly embezzlements.

The offworlders having an amulet explained everything— why Commander Tureg hadn't been able to find them, how they'd been able to abscond with large amounts of money without getting caught, and how they'd managed to hole up in an abandoned warehouse with welded doors and no one the wiser.

Then Theresa balked.

What will I tell Sorkha? she wondered, knowing she couldn't reveal that she herself owned one of these very valuable devices.

How I wish Chabi were here! Theresa thought, having grown to like the tiny old woman in the first three months they'd spent on Earth together.

Dismissing those concerns, Theresa turned her heat scanner on the warehouse floor. Faint but clear footsteps led her to a stairwell, which like the outer door was welded shut. She stepped through the two-inch steel and ascended, keeping the amulet solidly tucked in the circle of thumb and forefinger.

By the time she reached the fifth floor, the trail was so faint she couldn't detect it anymore.

If I were in hiding, as these two have been for the last month, I'd hide on the topmost floor, she thought.

Oddly, the sixth floor looked completely empty, the only place she couldn't see being in the center, what looked like a windowless room with its doors also welded shut.

She stepped through the wall and into an arsenal.

Three walls bristled with weapons, on the fourth what looked to be empty mounts.

Theresa stepped to one of the armament-filled walls. If she were to scrunch down, she could almost fit inside what appeared to be shoulder harnesses. She realized that all the weapons were placed strategically for quick donning. Within minutes, a soldier could walk from the room with enough firepower to take on a fortress.

Why? she wondered. And why four such sets of weapons?

And where's the money? Surely they didn't spend all the money on weapons, not when they could walk into any armory and take anything they wanted.

Puzzled, Theresa headed for the stairs, not knowing how long her surveillees would be gone. Exiting the warehouse, she retraced her steps toward the Palace, waiting until she was a substantial distance away from the warehouse before releasing the amulet.

What do I tell Sorkha? she wondered, knowing that every time she used the amulet, she risked disclosing that she had it.

Why don't I just tell her I have it and be done with it? Theresa wondered, passing Kharkhorin, the infamous hulking domed complex inspiring fear across the Empire, site of terrible injustices carried out in the name of Imperial preservation and hegemony, base camp for the Altai Secret Service.

Now, there's where I'd go if I wanted a weapon, she thought, thinking the outlanders stupid for spending money on something they could just take. I'll have to look into weapons purchases, she thought, regretting now she hadn't taken a few minutes to look closely at the particular guns in the arsenal. I wonder if any weapons have turned up missing at Kharkhorin.

Klaxons blared and klieg lights blazed, the fortress snapping to life like a giant jolted wake by lightning.

Theresa Appaloosa was instantly surrounded, fifty blasma rifles aimed at her.

Chapter 12

Amber unpinched the amulet long enough to sidle up to Bati.

Eyes wide with astonishment, he smiled.

She took his hand and slammed them into a parallel universe, a thick curtain falling around them. She scowled at the spray now coating her head and ears, the latter flattening in dismay against her skull.

While chaos exploded around them, Amber and Bati watched with amusement, the amulet firmly between her thumb and forefinger.

Bati's guard called out, "He's disappeared! Number twenty-two has disappeared!"

Amidst the gushing water, other guards converged, peering into the cell.

"Shut off the main!" was heard in the distance, barely audible between klaxon blasts.

Another shout. "Twenty-three is gone!" And the guards rushed away.

Another shout. "Twenty-four is gone! Tureg will pack her bra with our balls!"

Amber frowned, dismayed. Someone was helping her and it was disconcerting not to know who or why. "What the hell, Bati?"

"Twenty-three and twenty-four are my old friends, Chabi and Mengu. They're being held here for the same reasons I was. Each encountered a young woman like you, half-breeds born just after we overran their planets. They were summoned to Earth in transpods but were thrown off course at about the time the Emperor died."

"And I suppose they each have one of these toys, too, right?"

"Oddly, they do."

"Why am I just finding out, blast it?!"

"My first opportunity to tell you, child. I only just found out days ago, once we settled on a way to talk through walls."

"Hey, watch that child remark, I'm twenty-four, remember? We'd better scatter before they're wise to us, eh? Come on!"

Amber didn't expect them to find her and Bati behind the amulet's shield, but she didn't know enough about the technology to say whether they had a detector.

It's their technology, and if they hadn't invented it, we Felly would be free and launching raids against the Canny and chasing them off with the tail between their legs and …

Amber sighed, the tales of the old days before the Terran containment having inflamed her imagination, her maternal grandfather, a battle-scarred, half-eared, gray-muzzled old cat having told endless stories of battles and intrigue, the legendary Canny obedience always their downfall.

Walking through the quiet chaos, Amber and Bati exited the building, the trek up twisting passageways taking time to traverse.

Once outside, they remained under the amulet's protection, the streets in all directions alight with the blaze of a thousand military vehicles on the lookout for the escapees.

A knot of soldiers stood clumped on a street corner just one block from the domed fortress.

"We're on the same side, I swear!" said a voice within the clump of soldiers, its owner not visible above the helmets and blaster barrels.

Amber and Bati kept going.

* * *

Kathy and Mengu looked at Chabi and frowned.

"She's with you?" they both asked the older woman.

The frozen figure surrounded by soldiers looked pretty pathetic to Kathy, the drawn horse-face, clumsy hooves, and rippling mane stuffed into the neckline.

The cowering Equy was clearly pleading with the soldiers.

"Her name's Theresa. She doesn't look like much, does she?" The Terran female named Chabi whom Kathy and Mengu had rescued from the underground detention center looked as though she was about to repudiate the beleaguered Equy. "But you know," Chabi added, "in spite of her faults, she's a real workhorse, used to slog through the sewers for ten, twelve hours per day, never flinched from the dirtiest of jobs. You ask it, she'll do it."

Kathy wrinkled her nose, hoping she never had the misfortune to encounter a human sewer. "Should we rescue her?"

Chabi wrinkled her nose. "I don't think so, but let's hear what she's saying."

Inside the veil of frozen time, Kathy and the two Terrans inspected the Equy half-breed.

"See, my amulet glows when I'm near her. That's how I found that furry alley-cat."

Mengu and Chabi exchanged a glance.

"I saw that," Kathy said. "What was that about?"

Mengu wouldn't look at her, except briefly. "Uh, well, we know relations haven't been good between Canny and Felly…"

" 'Haven't been good'? Nice euphemism. So I'd sooner wipe my ass with her hide than befriend that pussy, what about it? You gotta problem with that?"

"Well," Chabi said, "I'd think you'd at least consider how similar your circumstances—"

"Circumstance, Schmircumstance! I'm doggone tired of being reminded how obedient I'm supposed to be. You forget I'm half-human, and my human half is revolted at the subjugation that my Canny half has been subjected to, and if you think for a moment—"

"If you think for a moment," Chabi interrupted, "you'd admire the legendary Felly independence, instead of being so defensive about your supposed obedience."

Kathy whimpered at the reprimand, realizing she'd harbored a secret jealousy since discovering the Felly's veritable armory and wondering why she hadn't thought of that. "I guess we all have our strengths. But I don't have to befriend her, do I?"

"As much as it might help," Mengu said, "no, you don't have to befriend her. Or stick your nose in her privates."

"You ever smell cat piss? Rankest stuff you'll ever whiff. Worse if they've been at it with that catnip." Kathy sighed. "Not that she'd let me—scratch out my eyeballs if I'd tried."

"Probably," Chabi replied, gesturing at the Equy. "Let's listen."

Kathy unpinched the center crystal to let time move forward, keeping her other fingers around its edge.

"We're on the same side, I swear!" said the Equy, surrounded by the knot of soldiers.

"Tell it to the Captain!" growled the squad commander. "Common, bring the Equy in!" He turned toward the fortress.

Soldiers lunged at Theresa.

Being lunged through was still disconcerting for Kathy, her arms linked with Mengu and Chabi. She felt them tense up as the soldiers bound the complaining Equy half-breed.

"Commander Tureg will nail your foreskin to her wall! Prime Minister Occuday will grind up your balls and sprinkle them on his morning omelet! Secretary Baihatu will cut off your penises and dip them in salsa for an afternoon snack! Emperor Kublai—"

A soldier stuffed a rag in her mouth, and he screamed when his hand came away without a finger.

The butt of a blaster knocked Theresa silly. She slumped in their arms and was hustled away.

"Ouch!" Chabi said.

"They'll grind her up into dog food," Kathy said. "We'd better rescue her! Spare the dogs!"

Mengu glanced askance at her. "We'd better not. If she's really working for them, she'll be all right, but the question is, why? What could possible motivate her to work for them?"

Chabi shook her head, looking the direction they were dragging the limp Equy. "I don't know what happened after they captured me a month ago." The small woman looked worried, her brows drawn together.

"If you really think she'll be all right, then we should wait," Kathy said, raising a doubtful eyebrow at Mengu.

"I think she'll be all right. Come on; let's go see if we can find Amber and Bati."

Kathy looked toward the fortress, its solid, slightly-rounded wall and domed cap looking formidable. "If a bunch of Cannies get food poisoning, I'll be saying I told you so."

And she turned with them toward the abandoned warehouse.

* * *

The lights blazed down upon her, the smell of her own sweat and urine filling the room with a stench so thick she could barely see her surroundings.

Theresa wasn't sure why she had slipped the amulet into a hiding place as she'd set out from the warehouse, but now she was grateful she had.

And the soldiers had failed to do a body-cavity search.

There the amulet remained.

Where she couldn't reach it.

Besides, she thought, why would I betray that I have it by using it to escape?

Her arms pinioned to the wall, slung above her head by short lengths of chain, her legs secured to the floor at the knee, Theresa couldn't even explore the wound to her head with her fingers, the slight warmth on her neck sure to be blood.

She'd regained consciousness just a few minutes before, and she was sure her captors knew she was conscious.

Probably needed time to summon someone important.

She tried her voice. "I'd like to speak with Commander Sorkha Tureg, please." It came out hoarse, but thankfully they'd removed the rag they'd stuffed in her mouth.

And the finger she'd claimed along with it.

She sensed motion beyond the walls, but it was still another twenty terrible minutes before someone came in.

Tureg, who stopped just inside the door. "Release her, and then get her cleaned up. Who ordered this? Gazonig? Bring him to my office immediately." Beside her was her ever-present Murry, blinking inanely, dumb and servile.

Grateful for their ministrations, Theresa cooperated listlessly while they took her to another room, dressed the wound, got her in the shower, and brought her a clean pair of formalls.

"My poor little half-breed Equy, so sorry you had to go through this. How could they know you were outside at my behest? You must have been following those two miscreants and didn't know they were planning that raid. A shame the way those soldiers treated you, my little loyal one. I'm certain you'll show them your value to the Empire, won't you? Tell mama Tureg where they were hiding."

Nearly suffocating, Theresa told her just to get the watermelon bosom out of her face. Briefly she wondered why Sorkha was so solicitous. Proudly, she recounted how she'd discovered the abandoned warehouse using the pattern of robberies, then let Sorkha believe she had trailed the pair to Kharkhorin Fortress, confabulating that as the reason she'd not reported the warehouse location more quickly. "What I can't figure out is how they get in and out of the sealed warehouse." Then Theresa looked at Sorkha innocently. "And somehow they broke into Kharkhorin? Now, that's resourceful!"

"Too resourceful! Eluding us this long! Either that, or everyone around Kharkhorin is incompetent! But not you, my sweet," Sorkha crooned, "You've done a wonderful job. Listen, you've done so well, I want you to train under a special operative named Bolormaa Joci. He'll teach you to move in perfect silence, observe without being observed, and mix into any crowd. What do you think?"

"So, I'm being taken off the case?"

"No, by no means, just a little assistance in the field, besides, there's been, how would you say, a little nattering that's come to my attention, a few naysayers who've taken umbrage at the proximity you've had to my person. Bolormaa may be trusted with your most intimate confidences while I see to it that these naysayers say nay more. Just for a time."

Theresa frowned, wondering why she was being placed at arm's length.

"You and Bolormaa should lead the raid on this warehouse the instant you feel up to it." A slow smile spread. "What do you say?"

Theresa smiled with her, frowning inside. "Sooner than later. First a meal, then we raid."

Sorkha grinned and reached for a com. "I'll have him come in."

Theresa grinned back, feeling like a fool and not quite knowing why.

Chapter 13

"Look, I'll just take you back to the outer end of the Perseus arm, where you can pirate to your heart's content until the end of your days."

"What if I don't want to?"

Amber sighed. She stood on a street corner two blocks from the warehouse, talking with Bati about their choices. What she didn't want to do was endanger him further by having him hole up inside the abandoned warehouse as she'd been doing for the last three weeks. It'd been enough to make her pace the floor like a caged animal, and the quarters were so packed with armaments that she doubted two of them could fit, much less abide each other's presence for weeks on end.

"And what about these other two, the Canny and Equy half-breed? Doesn't it strike you as odd they came to Terra at the same time in nearly identical circumstances?"

"I don't like Cannies, and Equies smell bad," Amber shook her head. "I've spent nearly four months on this stinking planet, and if I don't find out anything more about the reason I was summoned here inside the next week, I think I'll go home and start the rebellion they're accusing me of starting."

"Fair enough, one week. And if you won't meet these two other half-breeds, then at least let me introduce you to Mengu and Chabi."

Amber sighed. "Do you know what it's been like for the last month worrying about your hairless human hide?"

"You didn't exactly put your claws to my throat and force me to come to Earth."

She frowned at him. "No, but I suspect my arrival at your pirate base prompted the Imperial raid."

Bati shrugged. "You didn't launch the raid, so put a cork in the guilt, all right?"

Amber shook her head, wanting to be shut of the matter. "You've got your freedom. I'm offering to take you back where I found you, an offer you're welcome to decline."

"And then what?"

"And then what what?"

"What about you, Amber? Whether I return to that forsaken moon or not, what will you be doing?" Bati put his hands on his hips.

Amber regarded him, a stout man in his early seventies, his figure lean, worn but powerful, battered and bruised but nowhere near defeated.

"I'm going home."

She waited for him to object, to argue with her against it, to persuade her to stay.

He didn't. But neither did he change his stance, expression or aspect.

She thought about offering her reasons, but didn't. He knew them as well as she. She thought about the humiliating existence that awaited her on the Felly homeworld, but knew she wouldn't find a less humiliating home here. On Felly, she'd at least have air to breathe. She thought about the amulet, the mysteries it represented, and knew exactly what to do with it. She pulled it out of her pocket and pushed her open palm toward him. "Here, I think you should have this."

A streak lit the sky and struck the warehouse.

* * *

Near the center of the Ulaanbaatar, Kathy listened intently to the two old friends getting reacquainted, happy to have accomplished this one small task. The remains of their dinner strewn between them, a single candle burning brightly on the table, the restaurant a few blocks from the abandoned warehouse, Kathy watched them contentedly, mulling over the decision she'd already made.

She looked up to find them both staring at her.

"Well?" Mengu asked.

Kathy frowned. "I didn't hear your question, sorry."

"What now?"

She glanced between them and shrugged. "I don't know. Now that you're safe, it's ... I'm ... " She sighed. "I just want to go home"

"What about Theresa and this Felly, Amber?" Chabi asked.

"Equies smell bad and I hate Fellies." She saw them exchange a glance. Kathy glanced out the street-side window, knowing they couldn't understand, not sure she understood completely either, but knowing already what she wanted.

Shunned and persecuted on the Canny homeworld, or shunned and persecuted on the Terran homeworld. With few other choices available, Kathy knew which one she'd choose. Whatever else was happening, she didn't want to be a part of it. The toy strapped to her hand was fascinating for its capabilities, but it wasn't anything more than that to her.

"What about the reasons that you're here?" Mengu asked.

"They're someone else's reasons, not mine. Sorry to have dragged you into this, Mengu. I'd be happy to take you back to the Arcturus loop. Now that you're safe, I'll be returning home, and this?" She held up her left hand, and then began to unbuckle the harness. "This should be yours."

A streak lit the sky and struck the warehouse, blowing the restaurant windows inward.

* * *

From behind the barricade, Theresa tracked the streak from orbit and watched the missile strike the abandoned warehouse. Behind her and Sorkha was an entire squadron of Imperial troops.

For a moment, nothing happened.

A bright flash and debris blew in all directions, the shock wave pushing her back like a giant hand.

"Death to all Imperial enemies!" Sorkha whispered vehemently beside her.

The squad commander ordered in the recon crew, their envirosuits impervious to high temperature. The heavily-armed crew marched toward the building several blocks away.

"Do you really think anyone survived that blast?" Theresa asked.

"Of course not," Sorkha said. "But remember, his honor the Prime Minister ordered similar strikes on Felly, Canny and ... uh, the Felly and Canny homeworlds, and somehow the rebel leaders escaped them, which is why I'm having the premises searched. They'll be at it for days. Come with me, girl, we've got a press conference."

Theresa followed Sorkha back toward the perimeter, where a platform edged in bunting stood, an audience of reporters and the apparatchiks of officialdom were gathered.

Theresa wore an Imperial uniform identical to that of Commander Sorkha Tureg, sans the elaborate field of medals that decorated her left breast—and sans the elaborate breasts. Theresa's breasts weren't small by any measure, but nothing compared to Sorkha's torpedoes.

What would she do with all those medals if she didn't have such gigantic boobs to mount them on? Theresa wondered.

Sorkha stepped right to the microphones. "Friends, Terrans, Imperial Citizens." Her face appeared on the sides of all the surrounding buildings. "I am Commander Sorkha Tureg, and tonight our intelligence services have located and eliminated two rebels who, had they continued to rouse the rabble, might have posed a serious threat to the reign of his august majesty the Emperor Kublai Khan and his regent the Prime Minister Cyrbodan Occuday.

"The Felly Amber Calico and the Canny Kathy Mongrel managed to elude authorities on Earth for four months, and might even now be operating clandestinely if not for the perspicuity and perseverance of the young woman beside me.

"It pleases me to introduce Captain Theresa Appaloosa."

Sorkha pulled her forward and shoved her toward the microphones.

The lights were so bright Theresa couldn't see anyone in the audience. Sweat began to bead on her forehead, and her tongue felt like a lump of meat in her mouth. Her brain wouldn't work and she was sure the billions of people watching thought she was as dumb as an ox.

"Thank you, Commander Tureg," she stammered. "It was an honor to be of assistance." Quickly, she stepped back and a reporter in the front now stood.

"How did you find them, Captain Appaloosa?"

The fact that she now had a rank was a surprise, and the fact that anyone found her interesting was a delight. "The pattern of bank robberies was what let me to their hideout. These weren't professional criminals with evasion of authorities at the forefront of their minds. These were rebels seeking to fund and arm their rebellion."

Another reporter stood. "What about their associates on the Felly and Canny homeworlds?"

Sorkha stepped forward and pushed Theresa aside.

Relieved, Theresa watched the iron-haired, missile-breasted woman handle the question adroitly. And the next, and the next. I wouldn't have been able to do that, she thought, Commander Tureg working the press like a political candidate.

Theresa backed away slowly, idly fingering the amulet in her pocket, the device unaccountable warm.

"What now, Commander Tureg?" a reporter asked.

While Sorkha answered, Theresa considered her own circumstance—newly appointed Captain and Sorkha's personal retainer, haphazardly having fallen in with the iron-breasted woman, an Equy native with the unbeknownst human father brought to Earth through a sequence of bizarre events, and secret owner of a powerful device that had helped Chingis Khan to conquer nearly all the Perseus arm and to rule over those domains for twenty-five plus years.

Yes, half-breed Captain Theresa Appaloosa, she asked herself, what now?

Chapter 14

"Remember!" Amber shouted from the rock outcrop. "Charge as one, fire as one, fall back as one!" She looked over the armed contingent of Felly, their blasters all raised to the same angle. It had taken hours just to get them to stay still, at attention, all in the same way. Their target: a phalanx of mock Terran opponents, sticks stuck in the sand with white cloths attached.

"Attack!" she shouted.

Fifty warriors ran fifty different directions, yowling raucously.

"No, no, no, no...!" She hurled the megaphone to the sand below. "Capitan Birman, get your people back in formation. Now!" Leaping from the outcrop, she landed beside Bati. "Hopeless! They're hopeless!" She hissed in disgust and walked off down the beach, her fur bristling along her spine.

Three weeks back on Felly hadn't lessened her disgust. On her first day, she'd discovered that her mother had been killed in the missile strike intended to kill her, the blast catching the transpod and hurling it wildly off course. The guilt, grief, and anger had been nearly overwhelming.

Despite her mother's having been shunned nearly all Amber's life, the family who had shunned her mother had been supportive of Amber, commiserating with her and helping her to deal with both the loss of her mother and the destruction of the life she'd thought she'd be able to return to.

Furious, and knowing now who'd launched her on this tumultuous journey—and tried to kill her on a Ulaanbaatar street, and then framed her for the murder of the welterweight champ—Amber had instantly embarked upon training and outfitting a cadre of the finest Felly warriors.

Forgetting that the very same reason they were such fierce fighters was precisely why they were impossible to organize.

Stomping away across the sand, the surf on one side, grass-covered dunes on the other, Amber paid no attention to where she was going, nearly blind with frustration.

"Hey, watch out!"

She leaped nimbly to one side to avoid running the creature over.

It stood just over three feet tall, grayish whiskers twizzling skeptically at her, small eyes on either side of a conical, comical snout, and its long gray tail laid out on the sand behind it like the trail of a long evening gown.

"Well, where'd you come from, hey?" Amber would've sworn she hadn't seen the rodent appear.

"Here all the time for those with eyes to see."

"Calling me blind, are you?"

"I'd call you deaf too if you hadn't heard me."

"Some nerve you've got, little mouse, calling people anything."

"As you've not introduced yourself, I'd have difficult time calling you anything else. My name's Navid, and you're the commander of that rabble there, aren't you?"

"Navid, eh? I'm Amber, Amber Calico. Have you got a last name, or is that it? Navid Namecaller, perhaps?"

"How very petty of you, but not undeserved, I suppose. Yes, you're the one, all right. He said you'd have pluck, but sharper with the claw than the tongue. Saw you on Terra with those claws sheathed in gloves. Didn't know how lucky they were, your opponents, not to be facing your bare claws. Navid is my name, but my surname becomes that of the person I serve. Allow me to offer, if I may, my personal service, Amber Calico."

Taken a back, Amber frowned, "Who said? Offer me what? I'm confused. Did you just plant yourself in front of me with the intent of offering me your service? As If I'm some Terran Conqueror?"

"Your rabble will have to be a bit more disciplined for that," Navid said, his smirk at the ragtag group farther down the beach twisting his whiskers.

"And yet you offer that service? To me?"

"You are the one."

"The one what? You're talking in circles. I'm honored by your offer, but who am I that you should offer such a thing?"

Navid smiled.

Amber had that sense again, the one she'd had when Bati's masks had fallen away on the distant moon, the rubble of his burning pirate base around him, his deep longing to return to Earth so apparent, when he'd been chosen the agent of Amber's arrival on Terra, that sense of "here I am again in the grip of someone's machinations," that someone sure to be the deceased Emperor Chingis Khan. To test her theory, she asked the rodent, "His Majesty said I'd have pluck. How did he know, having never met me?"

"Slyly done, Mistress Calico. All in good time. The question that I put to you is not a trifle one. Do you accept my service or not?"

She considered, the sound and smell of surf comforting, Amber relieved to be breathing unfiltered air. These were the weasel creatures she'd seen following around all those high-born Terrans, whose utter silence and ubiquity tended to make them invisible. Everywhere, always there, never questioning, never complaining, the Murry had been considered so insignificant, their short stature making them laughable opponents in single combat, that the Terran juggernaut had bypassed their home planet with nary a glance, as though beneath consideration.

Rather than being offended by the slight, the Murry had instantly ingratiated themselves into the Imperial bureaucracy to become slaves and attendants, offering their service to the upper echelons of the Terran Elite, Just as this spritely Murry was now offering her service to Amber.

She hadn't ever heard of them offering themselves to any of the conquered races.

Her half-breed status already set her apart from her peers, and the only reason "the rabble" had agreed to be trained under her tutelage was her fighting prowess. A Murry following her around slavishly was likely to set her apart further, especially on Felly, where the concept of slavery, like obedience, was so anathema to the Felly psyche that it either provoked instant rebellion or gales of laughter.

Smaller Earth vermin versions of the Murry had once been considered a Felly delicacy. "What if that rabble's only liking for you is dipped in catnip for breakfast?"

Navid pulled a short sword from his belt and grinned. "I'm a bit more mouse than they've ever catted around with, Mistress Calico."

"Stop calling me that," she said, annoyed.

"Back to the question, and again without an answer. As you're not appearing to hear my question, perhaps my calling you deaf isn't so far from the mark."

"Impertinent little shit, much more of that and *I'll* have you for breakfast!"

"You propose to eat me? Most unwise. If I may proffer some advice. For twenty-five years old, you've a bit to learn, I'd say. Now answer my question before I'm shut of you entirely."

"Do what you want, Navid." Amber snorted and turned to see what her rabble was up to.

"That's a bit of a problem, Amber."

Amber would have walked off if Navid hadn't sounded so sad. "Eh?"

"As much as I might bluster and threaten, I don't have much of a choice."

"What do you mean? Of course, you have a choice."

Navid looked out to sea, his whiskers drooping, his arms dropping to his sides. He sighed and sheathed his toy-sized sword, then brought his gaze up to hers. "I don't suppose you'll understand, as obedience, service, and devotion are concepts that clash with the very ethos of being Felly, but I feel I must try. Amber Calico, the reason why I don't have a choice about serving you is that I've been ordered to do so."

She was taken aback. "Ordered? By whom?"

"His Imperial Majesty the Emperor Chingis Khan."

She shook her head. "But he's dead! Why didn't his order die with him?" She was stunned that he even knew of her existence.

Navid said, "Because he ordered it in the name of his son and heir, his Majesty the infant Kublai Khan."

* * *

Kathy shook her head, as bewildered by the Murry in front of her at the implications of her assertion. "How would the Emperor even know of my existence? Much less devote a moment of attention? That's about as bizarre as my being summoned ..." She just looked at Orozca dumbly, realizing yet once more how enmeshed she'd become in the intrigues being perpetuated posthumously by the Byzantine Emperor. "So even if I tell you to nibble on your cheese somewhere else, you won't?"

"I won't," Murry said, a tear trickling from her eye. "Forgive me all my impertinence, Mistress Mongrel. Quite unlike me to snark at anyone, much less speak impertinently to she whom

I'm committed to serve." Orozca bowed deeply and kept her obeisance.

Kathy couldn't suppress her growl. Things had gone badly since her return to Canny. The first shock had been discovering her mother dead, killed in the explosion that had sent Kathy's transpod astray. In addition, friends and associates she'd left behind on Canny now spurned her, blaming her for her mother's death, further compounding her guilt and remorse.

It didn't matter that she hadn't detonated the bomb that had blown the police headquarters and the surrounding city blocks into oblivion. It didn't matter that she hadn't pulled the blaster trigger that had cut Professor Tossucan Aigar in half. It didn't matter that she hadn't misrepresented the killing as the work of an underground agitator from Canny bent on fomenting a rebellion.

It didn't matter that she'd done none of these things.

She felt she had, and the life she'd hoped to return to on Canny, pursuing her post-doctoral studies in particle-wave transmutation mechanics, had evaporated.

Despondent, hopeless, and dejected, Kathy had taken to spending her days laying on the grass in a city park and gnawing on bones.

Mengu's remonstrations had fallen on deaf ears, until he had finally given up and joined Chabi in exile on Sylvy.

For most of three weeks, Kathy had lain on the grass with other Canny derelicts, unwashed, wearing stained and soiled formalls, and gnawing endlessly and helplessly on bones, unable to stop herself, guilt and grief so overwhelming she couldn't face it, her only recourse to bury herself in bones.

Then this pipsqueak Murry named Orozca had approached and had offered her her devotion and service.

The Murry prostrated in front of her, the spectacle beginning to draw the curiosity of even the incurious derelicts who'd given up on life and had given themselves over to an addiction to bones, Kathy suppressed her growl, feeling pity for the puny creature before her, imagining the indignity of having to subjugate oneself to a pathetic osteoholic in shabby formals who stank of excrement and looked like something the cat dragged in.

"Look, you're making a scene, all right? The last thing I want is more attention. I don't deserve your service, and you won't find me pleasant to deal with, so you might as well go away now."

The Murry got to her feet and put her hands on her hips. "Give that to me!"

Kathy looked up, glanced guiltily down at the bone between her paws, and looked back up. "That?"

"That!"

"But—"

Orozca ripped it from between her paws.

"Oww! Hey! You can't—"

She did, hurling it across the park, where a pack of osteoholics descended on it like a kernel of corn on a henhouse floor.

Furious, Kathy leaped at the Murry, but she wasn't there. Sparks exploded across her vision, and Kathy rolled over once, the blow throwing her off her feet. She rolled to a crouch, hind legs bunched under her, ready to lunge, but no sign of Orozca. Kathy thought, she's—

The blow landed at the base of her tail, paralyzing her hindquarters temporarily. Kathy whimpered and rolled over.

Orozca's miniature sword was pointed at her neck.

Helpless, she began to weep.

"Just what I need," Orozca muttered, "a weepy drunk. Dear Imperial Highness, what did I do to deserve this cursed fate?"

Kathy commiserated, howling mournfully.

* * *

"Can you make him go away?" Theresa asked hopefully, jerking her thumb toward the troll sitting near the door.

The Murry in front of her wilted, whiskers drooping. "Alas, I cannot."

The short squat man, Bolormaa Joci, had followed Theresa everywhere in the last three weeks, ever since the missile strike upon the abandoned warehouse in the city's rustbelt. Further adding to Theresa's consternation was Sorkha's near-abandonment of her. She had not seen the iron-haired older woman once in three weeks, and her every attempt to find out what her next assignment would be had been politely and firmly rebuffed by the Commander's secretary.

"The Commander's not available right now."

"She'll call you she when she needs to speak with you."

"The Commander will contact you at her next available moment."

But no call had come, no new assignment had been given, and this troll followed her everywhere—even the restroom, if she hadn't thrown a fit when he'd tried.

Further, on two occasions, Joci had stopped her, stepping in her way. "You can't go this direction. You aren't authorized to go beyond this point." A pair of burly guards had appeared behind him to emphasize his order.

She had left the palace on two occasions, once to attend a lecture at the university, hoping without hope to see that Canny Post-Doc Fellow sister expound on the nature of time mechanics, and the second time to see a boxing watch, wanting to see that Felly pussy pulverize one of these disgusting Terrans.

Bolormaa Joci had followed her both times, unobtrusive but always there, always watching, never intrusive except when she spent more than five minutes using the toilet, hovering nearly seemingly twenty-four hours per day.

Her greatest frustration was not having sex.

It was while she was plotting to escape his notice and head for the stables so she could either mount Jimmy or be mounted by one of his steeds when she heard a knock.

Theresa was so startled by it she didn't recognize it as a request for entry. Only after it repeated had she said, "What's that?"

"A knock," drawled Joci, standing in the general direction of her attention.

"I'm not talking to you, dolt!"

"Pardon, Captain, Sir."

The irony was lost on her, the new rank about as comfortable as a garrote.

"And if it's a knock, don't be a dolt and answer it! Make yourself useful!"

And in had strode a gray-furred creature not three feet tall, wearing the Imperial house servant uniform identical to the one Theresa had worn when working in the stables, the creature clearly a Murry, his name Pilar, and his intent to serve her.

Bewildered, flattered, and flustered, Theresa had immediately looked at the troll listening intently just inside the door. And asked, "Can you make him go away?"

And sighed at Pilar's response, "Alas, I cannot."

"I don't need a servant," Theresa replied, knowing such a statement to be instant conniption for a Murry intending to serve.

The whiskers twizzling, the beady eyes blinked, and the Murry sighed. "Very well, Mistress Appaloosa, I shall await your disposition nearby until you do have need. Again, my name is Pilar and all you need to do to summon me is call my name." Pilar retreated to the door and positioned himself just inside it, his presence there a perfect match for the troll on the other side of that very same door, the two creatures of equivalent stature.

Theresa could have pulled out her mane. With her teeth. One follicle at a time.

"This is ludicrous!"

Her two watchers grew wide-eyed at her outburst.

Theresa lifted herself from her couch, stomped to the door, and took off down the hall toward Commander Sorkha's office near the Palace entrance, her own quarters unchanged since her induction into Sorkha's service in spite of her heroics and official promotion to Captain.

The secretary was equally wide-eyed, and then horrified when Theresa reared forward on her front legs and planted a hind-kick into Sorkha's door that split it lengthwise.

"You can't...!"

She already had.

Sorkha was just lowering her blaster. "Theresa, my child, how nice of you to join me. Come in, dear sweet one, come in!"

Nonplussed at the unexpected response, Theresa stopped in her hoof-tracks.

"Oh, I see you've brought our friends, Bolormaa and... I don't believe I made your acquaintance. Not very polite, Theresa, not to introduce your friends. What is your name?!"

"Pilar, Mistress Sorkha," the Murry said, bowing.

"Didn't you serve his late Highness the Emperor Chingis Khan?"

"Yes, Mistress, I did."

"And who do you now serve?"

"Her mistress Captain Theresa Appaloosa, Mistress."

Sorkha's mouth dropped open. Then she closed it and looked at Theresa, then back at the troll, Joci.

"When did this happen?!"

Theresa covered her ears, the screech sharp enough to shatter crystal.

"Just, just now Mistress!" Joci fell to his knees. "I had no chance to report it, Mistress! No chance at—"

Fried flesh replaced the troll, Theresa hurling herself to one side to avoid getting caught in the eddy of Tureg's ire. Climbing to her feet, she glanced at the pool of bubbling grease that had once been Bolormaa Joci. "That was quite the prompt response to my first request, Commander Tureg. Even before I asked it. Now if you could do the same to this other pest, I'll be—"

"You blithering idiot! You haven't an inkling of what this means!"

Wincing at the piercing screech, Theresa half-expected to see the blaster aimed at her. Biting her lip, she said, "Uh, what does this mean?"

"Tell her, Little Pilar."

"Mistress Theresa," the Murry said, its ears flat against its head, "it means that I have been bequeathed to you by none other than the deceased Emperor himself, his Highness Chingis Khan, and thus it is implied that you have been placed under his personal protection."

Theresa went cold, the frozen stare of Commander Tureg sending knives through her heart. "But he's dead!" she protested.

"It is his will."

"You must be making this up."

"I have neither the capacity to fabricate an untruth, nor to deny a truth spoken to me, Mistress. As Mistress Sorkha Tureg will tell you, I am biologically and neurologically incapable of deceit."

"I didn't ask you to serve me."

"You didn't," Pilar said, shaking his head, "but you cannot refuse."

"Why? Why can't I refuse?" Theresa was beginning to panic, partly because of the crowd gathering in the outer office, beyond the splintered door, partly because of the deadly hostility pouring in futile waves from every pore of the big-titted, iron-haired Terran commander.

"Because, Mistress Theresa, to do so would be treason, a crime whose only punishment is death." Pilar smiled. "But be not concerned, because from the present until you die, anyone who attempts to harm you is also guilty of treason and subject to the same punishment. Congratulations, Mistress Theresa, for surely you have been blessed."

The death in Tureg's eyes told her only that she'd been cursed.

Chapter 15

"I've been cursed," Amber ranted at Bati. "What benevolent God would put a person through all this? What did I do to deserve such a fate?"

And all he did was nod.

Fuming, Amber tucked her head between her knees, a growl escaping her.

Nearby, placidly awaiting her instructions sat Navid, his small black eyes darting back and forth between her and Bati.

"What about you?!" Amber railed at the gray-furred Murry. "Do you know?!"

"Fate is something a person is born into, not a state one does something to deserve."

"Well, blast it all to Hell then, why was I born?"

"Indubitably the question."

Miserable, Amber groaned and looked at Bati. She didn't have to grunt with disgust. "What do you think?"

Bati shivered visibly, pulling his formalls tighter, the day warm and no chill evident anywhere. "He once asked me that."

The Emperor, Amber knew, a distant look in Bati's eyes. "He was here, wasn't he? On Felly, the year I was born. Navid, you served the Emperor. What was he doing here? On Felly, one of a thousand races he conquered?"

"Conquering," the Murry said.

Previously loquacious, now laconic. Amber shook her head. "Half-breed, Terran father and Felly mother, launched in a transpod, the very means by which the Terrans pulverized their foes, let's not forget, at the moment of that Emperor's death on a journey that takes me to the very doorstep of the commander whose siege of the Felly Homeworld results in its acquiescence—note I didn't say capitulation, something we all know is a Canny flaw—with a device in hand that appears to be similar to that which the Emperor himself used to conquer three-fourths of the Perseus arm, only to be offered, upon my return to Felly, the service of the very same Murry who once served that Emperor while he was here on Felly." She looked a Navid. "Deny that you were."

"I cannot deny the truth."

"And offered that service at the posthumous request of the very same said Emperor."

"It wasn't posthumous."

"He personally ordered you to serve me!?" Amber asked, dreading the answer. For some reason, that disturbed her more than all the rest.

"Yes, Mistress Calico."

She shot Bati a look. "How would he know of my existence, much less take a hand in my fate?"

"Indeed."

Rat-face isn't telling me everything, Amber thought. Chewing the inside of her lip, she looked a Bati. "You're looking pale, old man. What is it?"

"The traditions and proscriptions implied in the Emperor's ordering his own Murry to serve another, pre- or posthumously, have consequences beyond those that are immediately apparent. For example, anyone who seeks to harm you now is considered regicidal, for which but one punishment exists."

"Huh?"

"You now have the Emperor's protection. An act against you is treason, and death is the punishment."

Amber felt the blood drain from her face, understanding Bati's sudden chill. "So it's clear he took a personal and active interest in my well-being. Why?"

"Indeed, Mistress Amber. Precisely the question."

* * *

Kathy felt wrung out, like a sponge.

The Murry had dragged her to this motel room, where for the last twenty-four hours the walls had spun around her like a centrifuge.

Her stomach gnawed at her as though trying to consume her from the inside out, and all the Murry would feed her was broth. She knew she'd likely vomit anything more substantial, her digestive system deprived of food for such a long time that it would reject anything solid instantly, as if foreign matter.

Her bones ached with toxins and her muscles throbbed with lactulose breakdown, her three week bone-binge inflicting its inevitable toll on her liver.

She knew the first twenty-four hours were the worst. In her tortured dreams, she had begged and pleaded for Orozca to let her have just one bone, just one gnaw, just one lick, and when denied in her dream, she had tried to bite and claw. Her nutrient-deprived body, usually the epitome of the warrior physique, her people as fierce a fighting race as might be found along the entire Perseus arm, had proved incapable of mounting an assault, incapacitated by the binge of self-indulgence.

Kathy looked over at Orozca, dozing in a chair nearby, sensing somewhere deep that what had seemed a tortured dream had been a torturous reality, that in her delirium, she'd done all those things she'd never imagined she might do, to grovel beg plead threaten and even assault the one person who was attempting to extricate her from the mire of her own inglorious miasma.

Kathy sighed, dejected at what she had become.

I might as well kill myself now, she thought, wondering whether to turn on the gas in the small kitchenette and asphyxiate herself, or tie the shower curtain around the rod and hang herself. She pushed herself to her elbows and threw back the blankets.

Orozca had even given her a sponge bath.

Suppressing a whimper, Kathy stood unsteadily, the walls warping but staying mostly vertical. The bathroom doorway tried to elude her aim but she managed to drag herself into it.

The curtain rod looked too far above the floor to reach and the nausea in her stomach pitched itself into the toilet bowl, quite without her assistance. She barely got herself turned around in time to get the affluence of her effluent to go in, too.

Weak, sweating, and barely able to hold herself upright, Kathy considered the curtain rod high overhead, nestled on each end in thick, sturdy cups.

Then she glanced toward the kitchenette, measuring the distance.

Well, if the stench of my own emesis and feces hasn't killed me, she thought, the gas won't either.

Kathy pushed herself to her feet and teetered, half-expecting to fall face-first into the wall. She didn't dare look at what she'd left in the toilet.

The shower curtain wouldn't stay in the same place, but somehow she managed to grasp ahold of it. The curtain rod was obnoxious in its insistence in holding onto the curtain, but loop by loop, she removed it. The satin cloth bespoke the luxuriousness of the hotel. Rolled up, it was as thick around as two fingers, the perfect size for what she needed, the five-foot length just right.

Her delirium-addled brain seemed to tie into knots much easier than the rolled-up curtain. First, she squinted with one eye, then the other, as though squinting might help her brain wrap around the task of making a knot.

Finally, she had one, resulting in a loop of cloth strong enough to hold up a horse.

She tied one end around the curtain rod, and then balanced against the wall on top of the tub edge, two feet above the bathroom floor. She cinched to other end around her neck as tight as it would go, feeling the constriction already to her airway.

She lowered her arms. Just step off the tub edge, she told herself. That's all it'll take.

I've lost my mother, I've lost my friends, I've lost the home I used to have, a terrible one to start with, being ridiculed as half-breed nearly all my life. What would I possibly have left to live for?

It'll be best if I jump, she thought, quicker that way.

Quickly, before she gave it a second thought, she leaped straight up, her head thumped the curtain rod, knocking it out of its sockets, and she fell onto the edge of the tub, onto her already sore tail, and the rod, pulled down by the rolled-up curtain, smashed her between the eyes, and then she fell, rod curtain and all, into the tub, one foot hitting the faucet handle, loosing a spray of cold water.

Orozca rushed in at the commotion. "You're not supposed to take a shower like that! What are you trying to do, get yourself killed?"

Numbly, Kathy nodded.

* * *

Shaking, her voice tremulous, Theresa rose from her obeisance. "Prime Minster, your honor, sir, it is an honor to meet you."

The face of Cyrbodan Occuday exuded evil.

Theresa thought she smelled sulfur. Maybe it was the stench of her own flatulence. Her guts ground, her hands shook, her pores seemed steamy, and she was sweating heavily.

Beside the prime minister, herself prostrated almost low enough to be held aloft by her breasts alone, was Commander Tureg, quaking equally.

"And look what comes with our hero Captain," the Prime Minister said. "It's a pin cushion, or perhaps a heretofore unclassified vermin. Oh, but it's a Murry! One faintly familiar as well. Come rat-face, what's your name?"

"You've not forgotten it for a moment, Occuday." Pilar said, "You know who I am. You know why I'm here."

"Of course I do, but it was a pleasure to insult you just the same. As to why you're here, yes, such a pity you'll have no opportunity to fulfill your obligation. On behalf of the Emperor his Highness Kublai Khan, I release you from your vow to him through his father, the late Emperor his Highness Chingis Khan."

The whiskers twitched. "Only his highness himself can release me from my vow to his father."

"He's an infant, blast you! That's why I speak for him."

"Then I will serve as instructed until he's of age to tell me otherwise."

"I'm telling you now, rat-face. You're dismissed."

"I don't recognize your power to dismiss me. You speak not with the voice of the Emperor, and you never will."

"You will remove yourself from this chamber, this city, this planet, and this Empire, immediately," the Prime Minister yelled. "To disobey is treason!"

"And to disobey the command of his Highness the deceased Emperor Chingis Khan," Pilar said, his calm voice in stark contrast, "is treason. I commit treason whether I stay or I go. Therefore, I will stay. Carry out your sentence, Prime Minster Occuday, for I am certainly guilty of treason."

"NO!" Theresa said, stepping half in front of Pilar, afraid Occuday would slay the Murry right there. "You don't have to execute anyone, and no one has to commit treason."

Everyone looked at her, relief on their faces, but bewilderment also.

"What are you talking about, half-breed?" the Prime Minister sneered.

She looked at him, felt the weight of his ire, many times heavier than that of Commander Tureg. "Your honor, I will go with Pilar and live in exile with him." She looked at Pilar. "Thus, you will commit no treason."

The Murry seemed to wilt before her. "Are you sure, Mistress Appaloosa? I am here to serve you, not you me. I would beg you not to do this on my behalf."

"I'm sure, Pilar. Whatever else your service to me is, it's clearly disturbing to these Terrans. Let us not disturb them further, and comply with both the Emperor's command and this Prime Minister's edict." She looked at Occuday.

"Your exalted highness, Lord Occuday, Prime Minister of the Terran Empire, Regent to his Highness the infant Emperor Kublai Khan, I bid you adieu, and ask that I be relieved from my rank of Captain and all the rights and responsibilities thereto be rescinded. Good day, Sir."

Theresa bowed, took Pilar's hand, and walked from the audience chamber.

"No, Lord Occuday," Tureg's voice floated from behind her, "Call it good riddance and be done with them."

Having expected a blaster shot to the back, Theresa was relieved. *I still don't know what the hell that was all about!* she thought, furious that she didn't understand.

Chapter 16

"What do I do, Mother?" Amber asked the nocturnal wind, the moonless night so dark that only the whitecaps were visible, the ebb and flow of surf soothing to her ears, the smell of brine and sand a comfort.

In the dunes behind her slept Bati and Navid, although Amber suspected that Navid never really slept, the Murry legendary for their vigilance.

Unable to sleep, Amber had crawled atop a dune and sat on its seaward side, the breeze funneled up at her, the wind-whipped grasses waving around her, their rustle mixed in with the slosh and churn of surf.

She called on her mother's spirit to guide her, for in the Felly legends, everyone had nine lives, though, in some schools, they were all lived in one incarnation, in others reborn into other reincarnations.

Amber sighed, glad she had this carnation, knowing it as ephemeral as a flower—just disliking the color and quality of her petals on this go-round.

"You will shed these necrotic petals soon," she could almost hear her mother say, "and the flower that will bloom will be remarked upon across the length of the Perseus Arm as among the most beautiful in a generation, and you will be exalted as the savior of many peoples and the bringer of peace to a tortured nation."

Amber woke, startled, the glimmer of dawn touching the horizon, like hope.

A glimmer of hope.

The savior of many peoples and the bringer of peace to a tortured nation.

Amber stood, buffeted by the wind off the surf, not quite knowing what she would do next, but knowing she would do it, not knowing which direction to go but knowing she would find direction as she went.

The journey, not the destination.

For the central questions in life are but two: Where are you going and who's going with you?

And to the extent that the answers were not incompatible bespoke the harmony one might expect. Further, to the extent that a person accepted the answers that life provided bespoke the grace and aplomb with which a person lived that life.

The answers to those questions, Amber thought, aren't really what's important.

More important than anything is to hold the questions.

To accept the answer given but to say, all right, that's one answer, one possible answer, and to embrace the multifinality of life in all its infinite possibilities and to challenge those questions to produce other answers, to say to them, "What else?"

To hold the questions.

To accept the answers, yes, but always to be open to additional answers if life supplies them.

Where am I going and who's going with me? Amber asked herself.

She turned and descended the leeward side of the dune, certain that she was going.

Where she was going and who was going with her were questions whose answers would come to her on her journey.

* * *

Kathy looked drearily at the creatures around her, not quite believing her eyes.

A Felly, two Murry, a Terran, and an angry Canny Innkeeper.

"Get the fleabag off my property," the innkeeper growled, his bulldog face adamant.

"The only fleabag is the property itself, dog-face!" the Felly said.

The bulldog Canny dropped to all fours, hind legs bundled for a leap.

A Murry stepped in front of the Canny. "Pardon my mistress, kind sir, for it's clear that her tongue is far sharper than her mind. Mistress Calico, apologize to Mister Terrier this instant, and thank him for his hospitality to our friends. Now!"

Kathy couldn't believe her ears when the Felly pussy not only apologized, but thanked the proprietor, and even bowed to him.

"Follow me, Mistress Mongrel," Orozca said, taking hold of Kathy's arm and pulling her out the door.

The bright sunlight caused her to squint, sunshine an infrequent thing for the last week. Drained, bruised, and depressed, Kathy wasn't sure what these creatures were doing here, only that they'd extracted her from the fleabag motel after a weeklong hibernation.

Her forehead was still sore from the curtain rod striking it, and her sacrum squeaked with pain at every step, but she felt a glimmer of hope, absent now the desire to end it all or even to drown her sorrows in bone-induced intoxication.

"You know these people?" she whispered to Orozca.

"Navid like me served his Imperial Highness Chingis Khan," she replied, the two black beady eyes glancing briefly at Kathy. "Though not at the same time."

"You served him when the Canny capitulated, didn't you?"

"Yes, Mistress Mongrel, I did. Thirty years ago."

On a park bench across from the motel, Kathy pulled away and eased herself to the wooden slats. The trees were thick throughout the park, and Kathy had a sudden urge to relieve herself.

She trotted over to a tree and lifted her leg. When she was done, she turned to look at the three new interlocutors who'd so rudely interrupted her convalescence.

The Felly was taller and larger than most Fellies Kathy had met, the fur thinner, the ears less pronounced and not nearly as high on the head.

The Terran was old, the jet-black beard and cascade of midnight curl all the way to the waist doing little to disguise the wizened face.

The Murry looked identical to Orozca, but stood a few centimeters taller and looked slightly broader, the male dimorphism giving him a little more bulk and height.

"Amber Calico," the Felly said.

"Bati Kochakin," the Terran said.

"Navid Calico," the Murry said.

Kathy's glance went instantly to Amber's face. She'd not heard of a Murry serving a member of the subjugated races.

Just as strange that Orozca would offer to serve her, the half-breed, Kathy Mongrel.

"You're half-breed too, aren't you?" Kathy asked, realizing belatedly.

"I am," Amber said.

Kathy stood, her body complaining. "I've never met a half-breed before." She stepped close to Amber. "Are you spurned by your people, as I am?" She stood six centimeters taller than Amber, her Canny genes giving her greater girth and bulk.

"They accept me warily," Amber replied, looking not at all intimidated by Kathy's standing so close.

A thought occurred to Kathy. "Weren't you boxing in Ulaanbaatar a few months ago?"

Amber glanced at Bati beside her. "I was."

"Beat the Terran to a bloody pulp, you did."

A small smile. "I did."

"What's it mean," Kathy asked, "these Murry, these transpods? You have a disk ringed in gold, crystal in the center. You probably don't know half of what it does. You used it to put an arsenal together in a warehouse, then used it to penetrate Kharkhorin Fortress to rescue this Terran. We are destined for something, you and I," Kathy continued. "But what? And why?"

Amber shrugged. "I don't know, Canny. I wish I did."

"Call me Kathy. I'm no more Canny than you are Felly."

Amber smirked. "Only by half. Call me Amber. Pleased."

They shook.

"Now, I know you want to stick your nose in my crotch, but I'm not likely to have such a good response to that."

Kathy laughed. "Rumor, stereotype. A way that we greet each other, no one else. Your crotch is safe from me."

"The disk does more than this?" Amber closed the circle of thumb and forefinger on empty air.

"Yes, indeed. But we'd better not bring them out here."

"A suite has been secured at the Canny Hyatt, Mistress Calico," Navid said.

En route, Bati asked, "Where'd Mengu go? I'd have thought he was here or somewhere nearby."

The other two exchanged a glance.

"Bones are intoxicating to Cannies," she said finally. Walking, along in further silence, hearing the questions that they weren't asking, Kathy sighed. "Yes, I suppose I could start gnawing on them again and become completely insensate under the influence in a relatively short time. I could."

Kathy saw them exchange another glance. "What do you want from me, some promise I'm not comfortable making, that I'll feel bad breaking, that'll compound my guilt and make it even more difficult to stop next time? Careful what you're asking."

Amber nodded and fell into step beside her. "We won't ask you to make any promises."

Kathy looked down at the smaller, alien woman and sighed. The sidewalk was nearly empty, the hovers whizzing past occasionally on the street nearby. Kathy's thoughts whizzed through her mind like a thoroughfare packed with thousands of travelers, all of them rushing to far away destinations. She couldn't seem to keep a thought in her head. *I know I can't disappoint them. I know if thrown a bone I'll jump on it like a hen on a kernel of corn. There's a kernel of hope if I ask for help, 'cause I know I can't do this by myself.*

Amber's arm in hers was a comfort, the younger woman watching her closely.

Kathy glanced over her shoulder. The two Murries each followed his or her assigned creature, and following them closely was Bati, his eyes darting side to side, as though he expected attack at any moment. His having operated a pirate base at the edge of the Terran Empire for close to twenty years had taken its toll, his base often ravaged by patrols seeking to interdict his illegal trade and pernicious marauding.

They reached the entrance, the Hyatt on Canny having seen better days, their people cast aside once the Terran Emperor had stopped expanding his domains, the hotels, restaurants, and nightclubs that had sprung up like some cancerous disease following the Canny Capitulation having rotted away like necrotic tissue once Canny warriors were no longer need as fodder for enemy cannons.

"Thank you," Kathy said to Amber, stopping just outside the hotel door.

"What for?"

"For not asking, and for allowing me the discomfort of silence."

Amber smiled. "I didn't know what to say, anyway. But you're welcome."

Kathy smiled briefly and looked down, not knowing if she could abstain from bones, the thought almost bringing a drool to her lips.

Amber led the way into the hotel and retrieved the key from the desk.

Kathy waited near the elevator, the sound of revelry from the bone bar drawing her like a magnet.

"Oh no, you don't," Orozca said, pulling her away, the tiny Murry pulling the bulky Canny probably pretty funny to watch.

Kathy looked around to see if anyone had observed.

In the elevator, the other four were quiet. Kathy kept her gaze guilty averted.

The kitchen/living area of the suite was flanked by a bedroom on either side.

"I guess that means I take the couch," Bati said.

"Very gentlemanly of you," Kathy replied, wandering over to the window. The Canny Capitol laid out below occupied a wide valley between two ridges a hundred kilometers apart, both visible from this elevation through startlingly clear skies. Having seen little of the sky for the past month, Kathy was struck with pleasure at how clean everything looked, at stark contrast with Earth, where even the midday sun barely penetrated the smoggy murk. Looking over the beautiful city, Kathy realized how oppressive Earth had felt.

She turned to find the room empty behind her.

She knew what was in the refrigerator.

What they kept in every refrigerator in even the cheapest Canny motels.

Sweat broke out on her forehead. She dug her nails into her palms. Her ears drew back on her head. A whimper escaped her.

"Orozca," she said.

The Murry answered instantly. "Yes, Mistress?"

"The bones in the refrigerator," she said, her voice barely a whisper.

"Yes, Mistress?"

"Get rid of them, please." And Kathy turned to the window and wept.

* * *

Theresa looked across the small landing pad on the forlorn asteroid whose only remarkable feature was a small sign with a beacon on top.

She stood next to the sign, her airshell shimmering, Pilar beside her, and she looked back over her shoulder.

The terrain behind her was just as unremarkable as that in front of her.

The boundary was as artificial as any, simply the place where Terrans had lost interest in extending their Empire further. They'd encountered no resistance, no enemy, no galactic feature so obstructive that they couldn't have extended their domains. They'd simply decided to put the border on this lonely rock.

There really wasn't anything beyond it, an asteroid belt, a planetoid whose revolution around its primary took several hundred years, and the vast gnawing chasm of empty space between the Milky Way and Andromeda galaxies.

The rocks in front of her flared with the light of ship engine behind her.

Their escort, the military vehicle in which they'd been escorted to the border.

Theresa watched it ascend and change course for the Terran Capitol, Earth, its engines growing fainter and fainter until she could no longer distinguish them from the surrounding stars.

"Good riddance!" Pilar said, looking up at her, his voice on the optimitter sounding tinny. "I half expected them to cut us apart right here."

Theresa hadn't given it a moment's thought. "I was sure they wouldn't. Prime Minister Occuday is far too careful to leave any indication whatsoever that he might have had a role in my death. I'm not sure I understand completely, but I think he wants to engineer as legitimate a takeover as he can. He'll be the next Emperor in spite of Chingis Khan's posthumous efforts to assure his son's succession."

Pilar's ears flattened to his skull. "If we think Earth's an ugly place now, wait until he's Emperor."

Theresa nodded and looked around. "Well, what now?"

"We have enough supplies to last us a month, and then we asphyxiate."

"Here," Theresa said, extending her hand. Their airshells crackled, trying to repel each other briefly.

Hand in hand, they stepped across the border.

Fingering the amulet in her pocket, Theresa concentrated on walking, the light gravity requiring them to shuffle. A normal walk would have sent them flying off the surface, which was disconcerting at best, and fatal at worst.

The curvature of the asteroid was quickly apparent, and Theresa realized they'd reach the most remote point already, and would be back at the landing pad before they knew it.

"This looks like a good place." Theresa sat on a rock, gesturing at the ledge nearby.

Pilar perched on the ledge and looked at her. "Good place for what?"

Theresa shrugged. "If that damn Emperor foresaw events to the last detail and made provision for those possibilities, then he surely anticipated this one and will soon have us rescued, won't he?"

Pilar looked doubtful.

Theresa looked around.

The jumbled landscape fell away in all directions, plain rocks looking mostly brown, its surface scarred with the scorch marks and pits of collisions long past. Overhead, other asteroids in the belt twisted slowly, their own asteroid rotating slowly, the system primary a bright prick of light amidst a field of dimmer stars much farther distant.

"You really don't think that, do you?" Pilar asked.

"Of course I do, because if I didn't, I'd turn off my airshell right now and get it over with. There isn't any way off this rock other than someone's coming to get us."

"What if you're wrong?"

Theresa shrugged. "Then I'm wrong, and I won't find out until I asphyxiate a month from now. Besides, how do you know I'm wrong?"

"I don't know whether you are or aren't," Pilar replied, "but it would seem prudent to try to get off this pebble before we find out."

"And imprudent not to? Perhaps, but I'm not interested at the moment. By the way, any inkling as to why it upset them that you'd been ordered to serve me?"

Pilar shrugged. "Their plans for you were disrupted by it, clearly. What plans those were, I'm not sure, but I'm fairly certain they wanted you dead."

"Why didn't they kill me long before?"

"They wanted something else much, much more."

Theresa frowned. "What do you suppose that was?"

Pilar shrugged again. "Did you notice the way they had the debris from the warehouse sifted ever so carefully?"

"Looking for something, weren't they?"

Pilar just looked at her.

"All right, so, what are you wanting me to think?"

"Very well, I'll be more direct. What if they had the debris searched and delayed killing you for precisely the same reason?"

She fingered the amulet in her pocket. "It wasn't enough for them to kill the two rebels, was it?"

"No, it wasn't."

"They both had one, didn't they? A gold-ringed porcelain disk with a crystal at the center."

"I'm not sure, but based on what's happened thus far—if all those other events happened the way you described them, then it stands to reason, doesn't it?"

"He's got one, you know."

"The Prime Minister? Of course, he does. He has the original one, made for the Emperor by Professor Tossucan Aigar."

"Who?"

"The theorist who developed the technology."

"Wasn't he ..."

"Killed by Kathy Mongrel, the Canny rebel."

"Shame she did that. How'd they get an amulet, anyway?"

"How'd you get yours?"

"My mother gave it to me, just before I'd been summoned to Terra aboard that transpod, you know, the one that went awry. She said, 'Your father wanted you to have this.'"

"Who was he?"

Theresa shrugged. "I never knew. Some Terran who came marauding through Equy, our planet one of thousands to fall to them in their conquest of the Perseus arm. I don't know why my mother fell in love with him. She rarely spoke of him, or of that time. All I know is she'd lost her father, her brothers, and her husband in the war to remain free. She had every reason to spurn the humans, but not the man who became my father." She sighed and shook her head. "When did you serve the Emperor?"

"During the war to conquer your people."

"You ever been there? Seen the Horsehead Nebula blazing in the night sky, its billion suns flaring so brightly that we always had light to see by? It's just magnificent." Theresa was suddenly missing her homeworld, yearning for the fresh air and the endless plains of rich, lush grasses.

"Yes, I've been there," the Murry said, "with my master."

Theresa looked at him, startled. "What? Really? I can't imagine his Highness the Emperor Chingis Khan having any interest in the Equy homeworld. What was he doing there?"

"He fell in love," Pilar said simply, his gaze unfocused, as though he saw the distant past.

Theresa wondered if the Murry became so highly affiliated with their master that they sometimes felt similar things. Certainly, the look on the Murry's face was similar to the look Theresa had seen on her mother's face when talking about her father, a dreamy not-quite-in-the-present look, akin to the intoxication of Equy might feel when chewing on the finest of oats, or a Canny on a bone or Felly on catnip—besotted.

"Fell in love, eh? Odd he should choose the Equy homeplanet to do it. Weren't very many humans on Equy, except military and diplomatic types, right after the war."

"He fell in love with an Equy."

Chapter 17

"Fell in love with a Felly? What in his Confucian bureaucratic red-tape hell was he thinking when he fell in love with a Felly?" Flabbergasted, Amber stared at Navid, the Murry telling them all about his time in service to the Emperor.

"Falling in love," the Murry said, an air of distain about him, "is an art form whose very nature requires a person to suspend reason. He clearly *wasn't* thinking. It didn't matter what I said to him, he couldn't be diverted, try as I might. It was quite frustrating. I was even more put off by the fact that he appeared to be enjoying it. Him, of all people! In love! It was ludicrous, and it was splendid."

Amber could see that Navid really didn't see his interlocutors anymore. Kathy had been showing everyone the capabilities of the transpod amulet, Bati on the com in the next room trying to find his erstwhile colleagues, Mengu and Chabi.

"It really isn't so far-fetched, you know," Orozca said, sitting beside the slightly larger male Murry. The two of them together, sitting on the green couch in the living area of their suite at the Hyatt, looked like two peas in a pod, the puffy couch nearly swallowing their three-foot frames. "When I was with his highness on Canny, he did the same there—became so completely besotted with this young Canny Female that their love affair threatened to throw the negotiations into chaos. Two of them couldn't keep their paws off each other."

Amber glanced at Kathy, who looked dumbstruck.

Kathy looked back at her.

"Couldn't be ..."

"Orozca, how long ago was the Emperor here on Canny?"

"Thirty-one years ago, Mistress Calico."

"Navid, how long ago was he on Felly?"

The male Murry scratched his head. "Twenty-five, I think. The Felly were among the last of the major races to succumb."

He hadn't said that the Canny were among the first to capitulate. "How old are you, Kathy?"

Kathy's whiskers drooped, her ears laid back, and a whine escaped her throat. "Thirty," she said her voice barely audible. "You?"

"Twenty-four." Amber stared at Kathy for a long time. "Bati!" she called into the other room.

The long- and curly-haired Terran came in, a com to his ear. "What is it?"

"You were on Felly with his Highness the Emperor, weren't you?"

He looked among them first. "Discussing something important, it appears. Yes, Amber, I was with him on Felly—he landed shortly after I negotiated an armistice. We never really did conquer your peoples—far too independent for that. Why do you ask?"

"He fell in love on Felly."

Bati looked to one side. "Well, uh, I suppose he did. Scandalized everyone, the way those two carried on, kept everyone awake most of the night, what with all their catting around like that."

"What did she look like?"

Bati frowned at her. "Well, a calico, like yourself, with cute brown and black splotches down her sides—"

"—A white spine," Amber interrupted, "with two black ears and two frost-white cheeks."

Bati blinked at her. "How by my barnacle-encrusted hide did you know that?"

Amber looked at Navid. "You've know all along, haven't you?"

"I have, Mistress."

"Why didn't you tell anyone? Why didn't you tell me?" Her claws slid from their sheaths. Her hair prickled along her spine.

"Forgive me, Mistress Calico, but he prohibited it. He was very careful in his instruction. Of course, I cannot lie about anything, but he was absolutely clear that I was not to tell you anything."

"In other words, he wanted us to figure it out?" Kathy asked.

"Yes, Mistress Mongrel," Orozca said.

"Figure out what?" Bati asked, looking exasperated.

Amber looked at Bati, then at Kathy. "That Kathy and I are half-sisters, and the father we share is his Highness, the Emperor Chingis Khan."

* * *

Kathy felt sick, partly from not having a bone to chew in more than a week, but mostly with the impact. She stared at her half-sister across from her, and her tears rolled anew. "That means she's probably our sister, too."

Amber nodded. "Our sister, the enemy."

Kathy now felt horrified, the thought of their half-Equy, half-human sister working for Commander Sorkha Tureg, the triumphant look on the Equy's face as Amber and Kathy's deaths by missile strike had been announced, the gloating that had gleamed in her eyes, the truculent trot to the microphone, the bravado in the speech, the cockiness in the stance.

"How could she do that to us?" Kathy howled.

"To us, her sisters!" Amber yowled.

"Stop it, both of you," Bati remonstrated.

Bewildered, Kathy looked at him.

"Neither of you know what she's going through. Have you spoken with her, walked in her hooves? How do you know this isn't a ruse perpetuated by Commander Tureg? How do you know she isn't being held captive and tortured to play a role she wants no part of?"

"How do you know any of that?" Amber asked.

"Yeah," Kathy said, having wanted to believe him, not wanting to confront another betrayal by a blood relation. Upon her return to Canny, Kathy had been ostracized by the surviving members of her family, her uncles, aunts, and cousins having shunned her for her supposed role in her mother's death. Without siblings, and not knowing who her father was, Kathy had been cast adrift from the pack. So strong was the clan that her sudden lone-wolf status had cast her into the deepest depression she'd ever experienced. It was no mystery that she'd turned into an osteoholic, drunkenly chewing bones at all hours, so intoxicated every waking moment of the day that she'd often not even known where she was. Kathy very much wanted to believe anything less painful than another betrayal.

"I don't know any of that," Bati said.

Kathy whimpered.

"Just as you don't know either!" he added. "None of us knows, and it's easy to rush to judgment, but difficult to suspend our beliefs. All I do know is that Prime Minister Cyrbodan Occuday and Commander Sorkha Tureg are both slimy as snakes and just as venomous. Their goal is nothing short of absolute power, and they'll both do whatever they need to acquire that power. You, you, and your half-Equy sister are all barriers to their absolute dominance, and they'll come at you with money, poison, and all guns blazing." Bati looked between them. "Any questions?"

Kathy frowned, barely able to comprehend the implications of being the Emperor's daughter. "So, who's the heir?"

Bati turned to look at her. "You are."

* * *

"Mistress Appaloosa, wake up!"

Theresa woke to shaking, saw it was Pilar. "What is it?"

"I spotted something. Come on." He gestured and scrambled to the lip of the crevice.

They'd decided to find a semi-sheltered alcove to sleep in, not knowing how frequently the asteroids in this belt collided or how often they were subject to meteor showers.

In their enviroshell, even a pebble at a high enough speed would be fatal.

Theresa climbed out of the crevice, following Pilar, the light gravity enabling her to leap gracefully from rock to rock. Pilar led her to the sun-ward side of the asteroid. The sun would have risen in about two hours anyway.

Why'd he wake me? Theresa wondered, annoyed.

"Look!" Pilar stopped and pointed to the horizon.

The asteroid belt was a jumble of various-sized rocks accreted along an orbital line. The asteroid they'd been left on was fairly large, perhaps a quarter kilometer in girth, but it was mid-size in comparison to its companion asteroids. Floating along this orbital line for billions of years, the asteroids had reached a stage of relative stability, each one at a comfortable distance from its companions, each spinning gracefully on its axis, to the point where collisions appeared to be rare. Unless disturbed by a passing comet of considerable size, each asteroid would go on orbiting the primary for another billion years in relative stasis.

Pilar pointed along the orbital line, and in the distance was a blinking ship of some sort. It looked to be two or three asteroids over and headed in their direction.

Theresa smiled. "See? I told you we'd be saved."

"Not so fast, Mistress. Watch."

A burst of laser from the prow bit into the asteroid in front of it, and robotic arms began to gather the sliced-off chunks. The arms shoved the chunks into a maw, and out the back spewed a fine glittery dust.

"It's eating the asteroid," Theresa said. She watched fascinated, as the machine dined leisurely on a rock easily twenty times its own size. "Why's it doing that?"

"It's a mining bot, a robominer, breaking down the rock for the metals inside. It'll make ingots of the metals and store them in its hold, and at some point, a resupply ship will come by to pick up its cargo—very likely another robot ship—and replace its full hold with an empty one, and then come back in another year for the next one."

"So if we can get aboard, we can jimmy something so they'll send a maintenance crew to fix it, right?"

Pilar looked doubtful. "If we can get aboard. Watch what it does with stray rock."

A piece tumbled away, slipping from the grasp of a robotic arm. A drone darted out, netted the rock and hauled it back, where the robotic arm deposited it into the maw.

Theresa watched, fascinated while the robominer chewed its way through one layer of the asteroid, turned back and chewed off another layer, and then another.

In the space of about two hours, it had gobbled an asteroid twenty times its own size.

Then it turned to the asteroid beside their own.

"Uh, what do we do?"

Pilar looked at her. "What did I tell you? There's no way off the asteroid. I'd put even money on the odds they knew this asteroid would be harvested soon. Further, I'd even give you odds that they approved the mining contract with us in mind."

Theresa frowned. "Do you really think they're that devious?"

Pilar just frowned back.

"I have an idea." She pulled out the amulet. "When the mining ship turns to this asteroid, we'll plant ourselves in its path, turn it on and hide under its shell, and then when the robominers surrounds us, we'll turn off." Theresa spread her hands.

"We'll just do it my way," Pilar said.

"Oh?" Theresa was miffed. "And how's that?"

"See how it makes a run across the width of the asteroid. All we have to do is step onto it as it's making its way along the side."

Theresa watched the robominer chew through one length of the asteroid beside theirs, then turn and chew back the other direction. "All right, but I'm keeping the amulet handy in case."

An hour and a half later, the robominer finished with the other asteroid. All that remained was a fine mist of stone particles twinkling in the dim light of the primary.

The robominer positioned itself, like a wolverine about to eat an elephant, and dug in, the mist of particles nearly obscuring the sun. The asteroid under them vibrated ominously, as they watched the machine make its first pass. Approaching the lip where it had chewed off a bit, Theresa looked at the giant machine passing much faster than she had thought. Tiny claws on tracks grasped the asteroid surface from underneath.

"Are you sure?" she asked, not liking the speed, the window in which they might jump plowed past them even as she spoke.

"It's going pretty fast," Pilar said, his eyes wide.

Then Theresa remembered how she'd accidently triggered the amulet at the Imperial racetrack on Earth. "I've got an idea."

The amulet in her left hand, she extended her right toward Pilar. He took it, and she pinched the stone between thumb and forefinger.

The robominer froze.

Pilar's eyes went wide. "What did you do to it?"

"I think it's suspended in time or something. Come on." She tiptoed her way through the light gravity to the side of the machine, Pilar's hand in hers, and stopped at the gap between robominer and rock.

Three feet in between, little mechanical claws extended from the miner belly, nothing else.

Theresa imagined slipping and falling in between miner and asteroid, and getting ground into dogfood.

"Well?"

"Well, what? I'm gathering my courage."

"Don't let go of me, don't release the amulet, and above all, don't panic."

"Easy for you to say. How am I supposed to do all three at once?"

"You don't exactly have the courage of racehorse. I wouldn't suggest that as a career."

"Keep talking that way, and soon I'll be pissed as a racehorse. On the count of three. One, two, three."

And they stepped across the gap and onto the hull of the robominer, the magnetized soles of their formalls holding them to the surface.

"Let's find our way in before you set this monster free."

Theresa nodded, following him toward what looked like a hatch. Various protrusions on the hull bespoke fittings and attachments whose purpose Theresa couldn't even imagine.

With one hand, Pilar turned the wheel, carefully keeping ahold of Therea's hand with the other. Pulling open the hatch, he looked at her, bewilderment on his face. "How about you lower me in?" he asked. "I doubt we'll both fit in the passageway alongside each other."

"Are you saying I'm fat?"

"I'm saying these passageways are built for humans." The Murry shook his head in disgust. "Here we are at the absolute outer edge of the Milky Way, and you think you're the center of the universe."

She followed him in, pulling the hatch closed above her. "But even the center of the Milky Way isn't at the center of the universe." She turned the wheel to seal the hatch above her.

Pilar frowned at her. "Even the galactic core knows that."

"Of course it does." Theresa's turn to look bewildered. She knew she was missing something. "Shall I release the robominer?"

"You know, just in case, let's find some seats to strap ourselves into."

They made their way to the control room clumsily, having to navigate narrow corridors with their hands linked, the passageways a narrow fit for her bulky form.

The one console chair was too large for Pilar, the other too small for Theresa. They strapped themselves in as best they could, hampered by too-few hands, five-point restraints, and ill-fitting furniture.

Finally, settled in and still holding hands, the display in front showing views of the asteroid that the robominer was consuming, Theresa looked at Pilar. "Ready?"

"Ready, Mistress Appaloosa."

Theresa released her grip on the amulet.

Klaxons sounded, and the shuddering robominer shuddered to a halt. "Intruder alert! Intruder alert!" Flashing signs.

"Now we've done it," Pilar said.

"See, I told you we'd get off that rock!"

Chapter 18

"Do you think we'll get her off this rock?" Amber asked. She and Kathy looked down upon Earth from orbit, their transpod large but still seeming tight with all its passengers.

Amber's head was still spinning with the implications of what Kathy had shown them.

Back at the hotel, not five minutes ago, Kathy had brought out her amulet and said, "Well if you do this—" turned her fingers along the rim—"you get a transpod—" one appeared in their hotel room—"And this—" she drummed her fingers on its edge—"will expand it to include the people around you—" the shimmering globe gobbled each of them at a tap—"and this—" she rubbed an edge with a nail—"will get you each a comfortable chair." Three rows of chairs in three tiers appeared, each chair but four looking proportional to the occupants.

Kathy had then looked around. "Anyone want to go for a ride?"

Sorting who would sit where had occupied most of those five minutes—the two Murries obvious, but the Canny, Felly and Terran not so easy, their physiques not terribly dissimilar.

Then Kathy had held up the amulet. "And when you do this—" she spun it with two fingers on opposite edges—"you can choose which part of the galaxy to go to."

The Sylvy homeworld appeared in their viewport, the hotel room on Canis Majoris gone before Amber blinked.

Kathy had tweaked their location with a series of taps, and they dropped in front of a peaked-roof cottage surrounded by hedges, the house alone on a continental shelf covered with thick, rich grasses.

On the porch sat Mengu and Chabi.

Bati opened transpod door and leaned out. "Well, come on, you two. What are you waiting for?"

The two delighted Terrans had clambered aboard, exchanging greetings with the others.

"Where'll they sit?" Bati asked.

Kathy tapped her amulet twice, and the transpod grew, two more chairs forming in the expanded space. She had then spun the amulet with two fingers on opposite sides, and the Sylvy homeworld had streaked away, replaced instantly by the dreaded Earth.

Amber was astounded that the process was completely without the sensation of motion. They had just traversed half the length of the Perseus Arm, and back, a distance of fifty parsecs, without the appearance or sensation of having moved.

"Uh, Kathy?" she asked.

"Yeah?" Her grin went from ear to ear.

"Could you maybe slow the instruction a little? Some of us operate in real time."

Kathy's laugh was a deep resounding bark. "Be happy to." And she held up the amulet.

"Maybe it can wait, Kathy," Mengu said, his face composed with his infinite patience. "Until we've rescued Theresa, at least."

Amber was glad he'd said something. "What we need to do, Kathy, is get as close to Theresa's position as possible without being seen."

"How will we find her?" Chabi asked.

Kathy showed her her amulet. "See this bright orange point? That's Amber's amulet. As we approach Theresa, the position of her amulet will appear on this disc."

"The difficulty will be eluding Prime Minister Occuday," Bati reminded them. "He's got the Emperor's amulet, and we should assume he can see where we're at in exactly the same way."

"How do we know he isn't tracing us already?" Chabi asked. Amber scratched her head.

"Because if he were, the position of his amulet would appear on our discs."

Glad someone was able to master the technical details, Amber looked through the transparent transpod shield at the Earth below them, the continent of Asia clear, and in the middle of that, like a muddy hole in a meadow, was Ulaanbaatar. A plume of exhaust hundreds of miles wide reached from Mongolia across the continent, nearly to the place called Europe.

In the twenty years since Emperor Chingis Khan had returned from conquering the Perseus Arm, his capitol city had grown in proportion to the Empire he administered, and living downwind from that thickly-packed mass of humanity had become more hazardous that opposing his conquest.

How do they stand it? Amber wondered.

"Everyone got an airshell?" Bati called out, waving an extra one over his head. "Money, rations, weapons?" He waved each overhead as he called them out. "Commander Calico, all ready and accounted for!"

She stood and looked upon her ragtag crew, Kathy's team to the left, hers to the right. On Canny, Kathy had shown Amber the basics of amulet control, and their plan was to take two teams into the Palace at Ulaanbaatar—Kathy, her Murry and the two Terrans Mengu and Chabi, then Amber, her Murry and the Terran Bati—and search for Theresa from either end, using the cloaking parallel universe component of the amulet to obscure their progress, with a plan to abort and reconnoiter on the far side of Earth's single moon if they should be detected by the Prime Minister Cyrbodan Occuday.

"All right, people!" Amber felt she could count on every one of them, despite having known them for just a few hours. "We're here for one purpose—extraction." So different from her sister Fellies—attentive, still, ready to move at her word. "Nothing else! And we don't need to stop and get her permission. We snatch her and leave!" The disorganized rabble of Felly whom she'd tried to organize on the beach was no match for this group. "She'll probably have a Murry with her, whom we take also. Remember, find and extract. Nothing more!

"Ten Shun!"

They stood as a group, four to one side, three to the other, arms linked, and Amber looked among them. "Let's bring her home."

* * *

In their four-person transpod, Kathy and her three companions hovered above the rear entrance of the Imperial Palace, below them the wide esplanade leading to the Emperor's personal racetrack a kilometer to the east.

The rear half of the palace visible, Kathy scratched her head. "Where do we start?"

A hundred rooftops slanted two hundred different directions—balconies, turrets, colonnades, and spires sprouted from random structures that looked thrown together by passing sandstorms. Crushed quartz competed with flagstone, stained glass with murals, fluted ceramic roofing with aluminum corrugation.

"Why don't we ask someone?" Orozca asked, standing at Chabi's shoulder, the Terran woman only a head taller, just over a meter.

A small Terran was leading a large stallion toward the palace, the horse dwarfing the Terran.

"The Emperor loved to ride," Mengu said.

"I'll bet he knows," Kathy said. She jockeyed the transpod to the ground to one side of the path just ahead of the horse and his rider.

"I'll ask," Orozca volunteered, "I'll be the least noticed among us."

Kathy opened the transpod door, and Orozca slipped from the vehicle. Kathy then slipped the transpod back into its parallel universe, and the three of them watched the Murray.

"Where'd you come from?" the jockey said, bringing the horse to a halt. The horse whinnied. "It's okay, Emperor."

"Just stopping by, looking for Captain Appaloosa, if you've seen her, Master—?"

"Jimmy. And just Jimmy. I'm not master of anything, much less my own fate. And Captain Appaloosa? I wouldn't say her name around here, if you get my meaning. Finally got the come-uppance she deserved. Blasted filly fornicated herself all the way up to the Prime Minister, she did. Insinuated herself into everyone's bed, but didn't realize his honor's tastes don't include females. What about her? Why're you asking?"

The horse whinnied again, and Kathy's eartrans picked up what the stallion was saying. "Served the lascivious filly right, getting sent away in disgrace like that. But she had the best hay around."

"Forgive me, Master Jimmy, but what happened?"

"I don't know, silly Murry. You think they tell me anything? I'm just a stablehand. Enjoyed her talents a time or two myself. What man wouldn't?"

The horse whinnied and looked at his rider. "So did I!"

"You too, eh, Emperor?" The jockey turned to Orozca. "Last I heard, she got a visit from one of you, little mouse."

"Me? A Murry?" Orozia asked. "What was the name, by chance?"

"Pilar, I think, maybe Pilaf, like the rice. I don't know," Jimmy said. "All I know is that it put the fear of Chingis in 'em, and they ran around like scared rats. Last I heard, she was headed for the outlands, banished at the Regent's order."

"Banished to the outlands? You mean the galactic rim?"

"Or wherever the Regent disposes of trashy women. Now begone, Minnie Murry, before I set out some mousetraps for you!" The stable hand Jimmy and stallion Emperor turned toward the palace, nattering to each other in staged whispers about what a slut Theresa had been.

Orozca scurried back to the transpod, and Kathy let her in.

"We'd better warn Amber, Bati, and Navid!" Chabi said.

Mengu was chuckling mightily. "I'll bet it put the fear of Chingis in 'em! The Emperor's personal posthumous protection program—and none safer!"

"Pilar served his highness the Emperor when I was laying siege to the Equy homeworld," Chabi said. "Twenty-six years ago! I thought it was odd that he'd have three different Murries in eight short years."

"It wasn't chance, it appears," Kathy said. "He was planning for his own demise even then."

Mengu put his hand to his chin, looking among them.

"Something percolating through that devious brain of yours?" Kathy asked, knowing that look.

He sighed, the older Terran looking weighted down with the world. "There is something I don't understand." He shook his head and looked at Kathy. "Why would the Emperor sire three half-breed children fully twenty years before he declares his son Kublai Khan his heir designate?"

"Wouldn't that engender a struggle for the throne between the four siblings?" Chabi asked. "Murry, answering me this:

Why did the Emperor fail to acknowledge his first three offspring?"

Orozca smiled, "The absence of a thing doesn't necessarily imply that it isn't there."

"Well, then how do we find out?"

"You always find a thing in the last place you look."

"Only in a uni-verse," Kathy said. "In a multi-verse, a thing may be found in multiple places. Or in a multi-place."

"A singularity?"

"Even a singularity has multilarity." Kathy knew suddenly why the Emperor Chingis Khan had fathered the three half-breed young women and the one Terran boy. "We've all of us operated on the assumption that only one person can rule upon the death of the Emperor, and what he was trying to achieve wasn't a monarchy but a quadrumvirate."

"A what?"

"A quad•rum•vi•rate, a government of four people." Kathy looked at the rest of them. "He wanted all four of us to rule!"

* * *

Theresa stared at the snakes slithering in through the hatch, her airshell sparkling at the sudden vacuum.

"You are under arrest for tresssspasssssing," one of the snakes said, Theresa's eartrans crackling at the sssss's.

"We're outside the Empire's territory," Theresa replied, "We can't be trespassing. We're from the Ming Empire, and you're under arrest for trespassing. Turn over yourselves and you ship, and prepare of the commandment of hostilities!"

One snake looked at the other, then consulted a device he held in his tail. "I think she means commencement. Yikes! She's right. Who told us to mine this asteroid, anyway? We give up."

When they both just stood there, Theresa snarled, "Well? Aren't you going to raise your hands?"

The look they exchanged clearly indicated they thought she suffered from hypoxia.

"We don't have hands."

"Tie 'em up, Pilar!" Theresa shouted, indignant they thought she was so ignorant.

The Murry frowned. "We don't have any rope."

"Surrounded by incompetence!" Theresa shouted, and she proceeded to tie the two snakes together.

Leaving the knotted snakes in the passageway, she climbed out the port. "Come on, Let's commandeer their ship!"

Pilar followed her aboard the snakes' ship. Squeezing into confines designed for bodies far slimmer than hers, Theresa looked blankly at the dizzying array of controls.

Pilar squeezed in beside her. "Any ideas as to what does what?"

Theresa sighed. "None whatsoever."

"Why didn't you say you were stranded and needed help?" Ragnok asked, looking piqued as he slithered up to the controls. His body slipped into a series of rings, leaving his head free to view the vidscreen, each ring controlling a different ship function.

"We'd have been happy to help," Garkon added, taking her position at the helm. As science officer and navigator, she told her companion where they were going, while he got them there.

"Well, we didn't think anyone was going to help us," Theresa explained, feeling abashed at having misrepresented their situation. "After his highness, the Regent, banished us, I thought for certain our goose was cooked. What? What is it?"

The two snakes had exchanged glances, their bodies flattening in what looked like dismay.

Theresa grabbed Pilar's hand and pinched her crystal.

Thick dark layer slammed the cabin around them, and the two snakes froze.

"I don't like the look they just gave each other," Theresa said.

"I don't either, but we still need their cooperation."

"Maybe so, but after being on Earth, I can't help but be suspicious of people. These two seem honest enough, but how do we know they won't turn us over to the Imperials?"

"We don't." Pilar shook his head. "Let's just ask them to take us to the Horsehead Nebula, and there we can slip away using that fancy toy of yours."

Theresa nodded. "Once we're within reach of Equus II, we'll be able to get where we're going. You seem rather dismissive of my amulet."

"The Emperor had one just like it."

"Which the Regent Prime Minister now wears."

"And you don't find it odd you should have one?"

"Of course I do. I just don't know what it means. My mother told me my father wanted me to have it, never told me who he was. I've told Chabi all about it. Why? What are you getting at?"

"I served the Emperor when Chabi conquered your people. I often accompanied him to places that no one else knew he was going."

Theresa had the uncomfortable feeling that Pilar was trying to tell her something.

"His honor the Emperor Chingis Khan didn't always rely on military force to subjugate his enemies. Alliances, treaties, armistices, and even marriages were part of the bargaining he would use to suborn a world. Or the promise of. Why there was one place where he schemed to fall in love with the king's daughter, swore he would marry her if her father would only capitulate to the Terrans as a vassal state. When the king refused, the Emperor ordered a slaughter on such a scale that the streets were awash in blood. The princess turned out to be pregnant, and so she was shunned by her people, who blamed her for the horrific conditions they were then subjected to. The wrath of a woman scorned is but a fraction of a man's."

All of that sounded terribly familiar, Theresa thought. She looked at the Murry. "What planet was this?

"Equy."

Theresa choked up and bit off a sob, knowing this iteration of events had been kept from her. She didn't blame her mother. How could she have known? How could she have resisted the wiles of the most powerful and persuasive being that the universe had seen in millennia?

She looked at the amulet, heard again what her mother had said, "Your father wanted you to have this."

And Theresa remembered her reply.

No wonder her mother had clopped her across the head!

A tear trickled from an eye. "Oh, mother, I'm so sorry."

Somewhere inside, she knew her father hadn't been a bad man.

Just besotted with power.

And the means to acquire that power.

Theresa felt like smashing the amulet to bits under her hooves. The ambivalence tore through her. Destroy the embodiment of all the suffering that she and her fellow Equy had endured, or keep it and risk inflicting a similar suffering on others?

"Your father wanted you to have this."

Her full-Terran father, Emperor of the known cosmos, wanting her to have access to the very same technology that had given him the means to become Emperor.

Her, his half-breed child by an Equy mother.

And now her father was dead, and Theresa realized that his death had triggered the series of events that had landed her here, nearly stranded on the galactic rim, accompanied by the Murry who'd served him, hijacking a ship she couldn't operate in her efforts to return to an Empire that she'd been banished from.

Her father, the Emperor.

Her brother, the Heir designate, enslaved in the grasp of a prime minister who'd usurped power and would likely eliminate the one barrier to his assuming absolute control.

And Theresa banished by that same Prime Minister.

Suddenly she understood what Chabi had told her on the occasion of their first meeting. "There are no accidents. You're here by design, Theresa. Make no mistake. His design. Always by his design."

And Theresa wept for the horrible way she'd treated her mother.

Chapter 19

Amber, Bati and Navid walked through the wall together and all three immediately averted their gaze.

"I'd rather not have seen that," Bati said, blinking rapidly as though he'd been blinded by a bright flash.

Navid just made retching sounds.

Amber just pulled them back to the other side of the wall. "I guess we deserved that, poking our nose into other people's lives like this."

"I didn't even know you could do that with a snake." Bati shook his head. "I knew the old battleaxe had some fetishes, but that's beyond anything I might have imagined."

Amber shook her head. "Come on, Theresa has to be close." They had been searching the west end of the Palace, checking what appeared to be the personal suites of high ranking officials, when they'd happened upon those of Commander Sorkha Tureg, catching her in flagrant dilecto ménage à trios.

"I knew I shouldn't have tried to read the menu at that French restaurant," Amber said, shaking her head. "Let's try in here."

They stepped into the next suit—slumbering Terrans.

And the next. And the next.

Each suite was decorated to the taste of its occupant, some of them in the traditional tus kiyiz, or wall hangings, others in the motifs of other indigenous Earth cultures, all of them opulent, the fabrics of the finest, the rarest object d´art.

"There must be a better way than this," Bati said, looking frustrated.

"Let's see what I can do with this." Amber held the amulet level, still encircled in thumb and forefinger, and took her right index finger to the porcelain disc. With a few swipes, she conjured a glow to one side, the sharp orange speck to the east of them. "This way," she said.

They walked through several walls, crossing a variety of suites, each more lavishly decorated than the last, each growing proportionally larger.

"Uh, for some reason," Navid said, "I think we're going the wrong direction."

Amber looked back at him as she stepped through a wall. "What makes you say that?"

Amber swung her head around.

"I know you're there!" Prime Minister and Regent Cyrbodan Occuday stood in the entry of his suite, looking at his palm.

An amulet rested there, a bright point of orange reflecting the position of Amber and her companions.

"Don't try to escape, because I'll find you," Crybodan hissed, his eyes searching the place where Amber stood.

He can't see me! Amber realized, she and her two companions veiled by the interstitial transpod field. Kathy had told her to expect something like this, but with Theresa, not with the Prime Minster.

"Stay calm," Bati said. "He can't see or hear us. The only reason he knows we're here is because of that!" He pointed to Occuday's palm. "Which he stole from his Majesty the Emperor Chingis Khan. Traitor!" he yelled, a vein popping out under the skin at his temple. "Traitor!"

Amber restrained him. "Now's not the time, Bati, but soon!"

"Soon I'll get you!" Cyrbodan yelled in their direction. "I'll hunt you down and eliminate you just as I did your horse-faced sister! Are you that mongrel daughter, or the scaredy-cat one? No matter, I'll hound you both until you beg me to spare you!"

"Let him rant," Navid said, pulling on Amber's arm. "Let's go. The longer we stay, the more we feed on his grandiose cupidity and paranoia."

Amber nodded, stepping backward through the wall. The amber point of light on her amulet blinked out. "Where'd he go?" Just to be safe, she pinched the crystal in the center, stopping time.

"We'd better get going before he comes after us," Bati said.

Amber agreed. She remembered Kathy telling her that once time was frozen, they were just as invisible to the people around them as when under the umbrella of a parallel universe. Then Kathy had described how to use the translation tool, the distance compression function of the transpod actuator.

The crystal pinched, Amber swiped her forefinger from the inner disk edge to the outer. They rocketed out of the palace and hovered above the Earth.

"Look out!" Navid yelled, hands over his head.

A comet hung suspended a meter away from them; its trajectory, had it been moving, would have wiped them out.

"Where'd that come from?" Amber said, looking at the amulet.

On the porcelain disk an orange dot arced toward them.

Amber shoved her fingertip across the disk, and they lurched across the Solar System.

"Quick, the matter activator!"

She shot Bati a look, then twisted the gold band encircling the porcelain disk. The Milky Way shrank to a pinpoint, the crystal growing hot under her fingers.

"Other way, sorry," Bati said, grinning sheepishly.

She reversed the move, reducing the three of them to a pinpoint. The umbra thick around them, light not about to reach them, Amber wondered if they'd be safe while microscopic.

The disk stayed blank, Amber, Bati, and Navid looking at each other nervously.

"Made ourselves so small he can't find us, I gather?" Navid ventured, wincing as though pained.

Bati nodded. "Mengu knows the dynamics of interstitial mechanics better than I do, but the main question is whether the link between amulets is always active, or can it be disrupted by change-of-states?"

"We still need to find Theresa, though."

"Which we can't do while we're under attack. Occuday won't give up either. I suspect he knows as much as Mengu about the amulets, probably more."

Amber frowned. "It'll take all three of us together to defeat him."

"His Highness the Emperor Chingis Khan planned that you could."

She looked at him. "I'm getting annoyed with his Highness, because we have to find Kathy first."

* * *

"We have to find Amber first," Kathy said, scanning the rooftops of the sprawling palace below, as though she might locate Amber and crew by looking at roofs.

"That's a bizarre looking structure," Orozca said, pointing southward.

Kathy looked to port, saw the cooper roof, what looked like a perfect hemisphere at least three meters in diameter.

The hemisphere warped and shuddered, as though liquefying.

"Did you see that?" Kathy asked.

"See what?" Orozca looked at her, her brows drawn together.

"You were looking right at it. How couldn't you have seen it?"

"Seen what?" The Murry frowned. "Are you feeling all right?"

"Of course I am. The Copper dome. You didn't see it deform, as though it turned to liquid?"

Orozca shook her head.

"Let's go see," Kathy said, and she brought their transpod over to the copper dome and lowered them through the roof.

Below was a luxurious apartment, suites carpeted in the finest satin rugs of electrifying design, walls papered with shimmering fabrics, statuettes of the purest marble, gilded lintels and doorposts, silk embroidered chairs and footstools.

"Luxury fit for a king." Mengu muttered.

"Or a Regent Prime Minister," Kathy snickered.

Orozca stuck her nose in the air. "Smell that?"

Kathy sampled it as well. The unmistakable stench of a frightened Terran, her bloodhound nose locking instantly on how fresh the scent was. "And he just left—scared, badly scared." She and Mengu exchanged a glance.

"Maybe you saw him leaving," Orozca said.

She and Mengu looked at the Murry.

"In a transpod," the mousy woman added.

"Why would I be able to see something that you can't?"

"You have the amulet," Orozca said matter of factly.

"Amber!" Mengu said. "He saw Amber—and he's going after her! Kathy, your amulet!"

On the surface of the disk, two orange points rocketed toward each other, then one winked out just before they collided. The remaining point changed course and headed toward them.

"Quick, the matter actuator!"

Kathy was already twisting, and the room expanded, growing rapidly larger, and they disappeared into the carpet, one speck of dust among billions.

"Now, the time deactivator."

She pinched the crystal, having to suspend their interstitial shift to a parallel universe. She had not yet mastered the technique of using all three interstitial dimensions of time, matter, and distance.

Time froze, their aspect so small—measured in microns—that the other amulet user would have had to occupy the molecule beside them for the orange point of light to appear on the porcelain disk.

"I think we're safe for now," Orozca said.

"Safe in the jaws of the lion," Mengu muttered.

"Safe until we try to escape," Kathy added, frowning at her two companions.

* * *

Theresa sat on the hull wrapped in her airshell, the ship streaking toward the Horsehead Nebula and her homeworld, Equy.

Unconcerned that a passing speck of space dust might perforate her and abruptly end her life.

The Horsehead Nebula coming into view, Theresa shifted to a kneeling position and bowed her head.

"Oh Great Father, King of your skies, Patron of our race, Protector of our domains, help this hapless hopeless helpless halfling Equy to decide what to do, and forgive me my Terran blood, which I did not ask for and would renounce if I might simply cast that half away.

"Oh Great Father, help me, for I know not what to do.

"Help me know how to use this gift given by the terrible Terran who fathered me.

"Help me to throw it into the volcanoes of doom if that is your will.

"Help me to help my sisters, whom I have unjustly pursued at the behest of my enemy, man.

"Help me to forgive myself my odious deeds.

"Help me to forgive my fillyandering with man, beast, and Equy alike.

"Help me, Great Father, to redeem myself in the eyes of my sisters, who deserve not the betrayal I inflicted upon them, in my ignorance. Help me to see where I am ignorant still, and give me the strength to be gentle and wise with myself, for I surely have been merciless and ill-advised toward others.

"Help me, Great Father, King of our skies, Patron of our race, Protector of our domains, please, I beg you to help me."

And Theresa wept.

The hand on her arm was a comfort, but still she wept.

The ship hove into orbit above the Equy homeworld.

"And help my people, to whom I might have been princess, help them forgive me." And she burst into tears again.

Along time later, the small Murry's hand still on her arm, the snake miner-repair ship quiescent under her, Theresa wiped the tears away and sighed.

"Did you know my mother, Pilar?"

"I did, Mistress Appaloosa."

"What was she like?"

"She was as beautiful as midnight, a charcoal-black filly who strutted with more dignity and grace than her father the Equy King might expect. Her flanks shimmered when she walked and she turned heads from the moment she foaled, heads of men and women alike. And in her spirit was all the compassion and empathy that a people would want from their Queen. She was majestic."

Theresa tried to imagine her mother before she became pregnant by the Terran Emperor. She failed utterly.

All she knew was the dumpy, dejected mare with the sagging stomach and plodding gait of a thoroughly demoralized creature, not the proud highborn thoroughbred whom she had been.

"And most of all, Great Father," Theresa said toward the Horsehead Nebula hovering in the skies above her natal planet, "Most of all, help my mother to forgive me, just as I pray for the grace to forgive her."

That, Theresa thought, if nothing else, that. Let us forgive each other, me and my Dam.

Sighing, Theresa looked at Pilar. "Thank you, my friend."

"It's my pleasure to serve, Mistress."

She smiled. "Let's go see my mother."

Chapter 20

Amber smiled, looking down on the Equy homeworld, seeing an orange speck on the porcelain disk. "She's there, all right." Earlier, hovering above Earth, trying to make themselves so small that Cyrbodan Occuday couldn't see them, Amber had looked at her disk and had seen that the Prime Minister was gone.

Their ploy had worked.

Then Bati had suggested that the amulet might have a setting for the breadth of its other-amulet sensor.

"Well, how do I adjust it, then?" Amber had asked.

Navid had promptly answered.

"You knew all along?"

"Of course."

"Why didn't you say something?"

He'd looked at them blankly. "I was just waiting to be asked."

Bati had restrained Amber from filleting the Murry. "That's their nature."

The easy way to locate my sister, Amber was thinking, and the little rat let us put ourselves in danger before telling us about it. She looked down on the Equy homeworld, the Horsehead Nebula looming nearby like a stallion guarding the herd

As Bati had pointed out, none of them had thought to ask.

"Come on, what are we waiting for?" Bati asked.

"Let's go." Amber adjusted the amulet, and they dropped to the planet surface.

Equal parts land and sea, Equy was humid, the air thick with moisture and aromatic with flora. Grasslands carpeted gently rolling hills, dotted with copses of trees, the terrain without evident mountain ranges beyond a few thousand meters, thick deciduous forests covering those, and everywhere the succulent grasses.

Where Amber and crew disembarked was a cemetery perched on the continental shelf, below them a gentle sea. Northward along the coast glittered a crystal city, multiple spines glistening as they reached into the sky. Just inland from that was the flare of a starliner descending to the spaceport.

The cemetery abutted a stand of oak, standing sentinel over its mournful charge.

"What are we doing here?" Bati said.

Amber pointed to a lone Equy just visible near the back of the graveyard, beside her a Murry, the gray-furred creature nearly blending in with the headstones. Amber looked at the sign standing beside the graveyard entrance, a slab of granite with indecipherable characters on it. Equy, of course, Amber thought.

"Here lie our valiant warriors, fallen to the onslaught inflicted upon us by the Terran menace," Bati translated.

They entered the cemetery, passing row after row of headstone, at least five kilometers between the precipice to the sea and the oaks standing sentinel. The headstones, Amber realized, were spaced no farther apart than needed for a full grown Equy to pass between them.

She tried to estimate how many were here, and her mind stumbled over the enormity.

It took a long time to reach the far edge.

Amber stopped several rows away.

The Equy female, who looked small for her species, stood at the very last row over a headstone that appeared whiter that its fellows, less weather-worn, the grass at its base newer.

Navid went ahead and greeted the Murry standing beside the Equy.

Amber and Bati waited respectfully at a distance, Amber blinking back tears, knowing what she beheld, the fresh grief over her own mother's loss just below the surface.

She likely just found out, Amber thought, guessing Theresa had not been back to Equy since departing in a transpod gone awry.

The Equy turned, her face a wreck.

Amber was surprised how close to Terran it looked, compared with a full-blooded Equy.

Teresa wouldn't look at her, didn't approach her, remained standing beside the grave of her mother.

"Sister," Amber said softly, "may I come near?"

The woman's glance came up once then returned to her feet. And then she nodded.

Amber stepped toward her, seeing in Teresa's face not just disconsolate sorrow but also horrific guilt. Survivor's guilt, just like Amber felt, but something more, something feral.

She tried to kill me, Amber remembered, and feels terrible about it. "They deceived you, Theresa. They lied to you to turn you against your sisters."

"Can you ever forgive me?" Theresa wailed, tears bursting anew from cried-out eyes, sobs wrenching from sob-wrenched lungs, cries croaking from a cry-hoarsened throat.

Amber stepped up to the big woman and slipped her arms around her sister's waist. "Of course, I forgive you," she said, her half-Equy half-sister a half-meter taller than her. "Of course, I forgive you."

Amber held Theresa until she'd exhausted her tears, the day growing long as the sisters stood at the edge of a cemetery perched on the edge of a continent.

The sun hovered above the horizon when Theresa pulled away. She kept apologizing, which Amber knew wasn't necessary but didn't mind, glad to have her sister near, realizing this was one creature at least who would never insult her for her half-breed status, their sisterhood stronger for the shared experience of having been shunned by their respective races.

Acceptance had been rare for Amber. Larger than most Felly, she had always stood out, her difference emphasized by her relatively sparse fur, small ears, flat face, and muscular bulk. Only her mother and for a brief time the Welterweight Champ Terran McFall had accepted Amber for precisely who she was.

Well, Bati and Navid, too.

She looked up at Theresa, seeing some characteristics in her face that reminded her of Kathy. "You have another sister, you know."

Theresa nodded glumly. "Will Kathy forgive me?"

Amber smiled. "Of course she will, but there is another whose forgiveness you'll have the most difficulty with, someone more dear to you than you'll ever know."

"Chabi?" The look on Theresa's face indicated she knew that wasn't the answer.

"No, not Chabi," Amber said, taking Theresa's hoof in both of her paws. "How will Theresa forgive you?"

As Theresa wept anew, Amber wept with her, knowing that to be the challenge each of them would find the most difficult.

* * *

Kathy looked around the room, tongue lolling out with happy panting, vestigial tail wagging rapidly, ecstatic to have everyone in the same room.

Three Murries, three Terrans, and three half-breed sisters had finally managed to collect in one place.

"I suppose as the eldest and most obedient of the three sisters, I should preside over our gathering," she said, unable to suppress her grin.

"Have I been disobedient?" Amber protested immediately.

"My middle name is wanton," Theresa muttered, whinnying softly and looking sheepish, a rather difficult accomplishment for an Equy.

"The past is past, sister. It's all about the future now." Kathy grinned at her, happy to have finally met the wayward one. Glancing over at Mengu, Kathy nodded.

A picture flashed onto the wall behind her.

"Around the neck of our late father the Emperor Chingis Khan is an amulet," Kathy said. "A gold ring around a porcelain disk, a crystal embedded in the center. At the heart of the disk is a miniaturized transpod activator, a device that allows its user to access the interstitial fields created by the transmutation of light, matter, and distance between their wave and particle states."

"My brain hurts already," Amber said.

"Mastery of the science itself and the terminology isn't required to use the device."

"Isn't there a simpler way to use it, though?" Theresa asked. "My hooves don't articulate quite well enough to use the amulet."

"Of course there is," Pilar said, sitting between Navid and Orozca, the three Murries sitting so quaintly in a row that Kathy automatically added dark glasses and canes.

She couldn't suppress a giggle. "Tap the crystal three times thus—" she tapped in a measured rhythm, and a still of the controls appeared on the wall—"will put you at these controls inside the transpod. Since his Highness didn't want to be so conspicuous as to disappear right in front of others, he developed the fine-motor interface, enabling him to use a simple gesture to shift himself into timelessness or elsewhere." Kathy signaled to Mengu. "As in this Empire-wide address."

A vid of the Emperor before the Mongolian House of Yurts showed him placing his hand delicately at the base of his throat and then dropping it again.

"If you'll notice on the replay, his cravat is tucked quite a bit farther in after he lowers his hand." It was the only place in the vid indicating some discrepancy.

"He truly was the Emperor who was everywhere at once." Kathy saw her sisters exchange a glance. "Now, perhaps we sisters aren't too happy about his methods—I can certainly attest to the grief I've experienced, and I'll attempt not to excuse it—but he also gave us the means to remediate some of the suffering he inflicted.

"Professor Tussucan Aigar, whom I purportedly killed, extracted a promise from his Highness the Emperor—to give the conquered races an opportunity to participate in the governing of the Empire. It's unfortunate he wasn't more specific as to the means of doing so, but our having an amulet gives each of us the opportunity to secure for our people the self-determination we each badly need.

"Theresa," Kathy said, looking directly at her half-Equy sister, "tell us about the Emperor's attempt to integrate your homeworld into the Empire before hostilities commenced."

Theresa looked down, her face suddenly sad. "My grandfather, King Haggen Appaloosa, was considering a request by the Emperor Chingis Khan to marry my mother, Angelina. As with any courtship, the two met on many occasions while the betrothal was being negotiated. When the talks broke down because King Haggen was adamant about retaining some autonomy within his own domains around the Horsehead Nebula, Emperor Chingis Khan declared war rather than cede, but my mother was already pregnant, and perhaps because of that perceived betrayal, neither the Emperor Chingis Khan nor my grandfather, King Haggen Appaloosa, could be persuaded to relinquish their intransigent positions, and the slaughter was horrific."

Two chairs over, her head buried in Mengu's shoulder, Chabi was weeping softly.

Theresa rose and sat beside her, and enfolded her in her ample arms. The small Terran in the embrace of the large half-breed whose people she had slaughtered brought Kathy to the edge of tears.

"I fear that our trying to obtain our independence will engender much more sorrow." Kathy looked at Amber, Canny at Felly, two races that had warred incessantly with each other. "And we two will certainly revert to our previously contentious ways, in spite of any intention we might have otherwise."

"Perhaps you might obtain your people's obedience in respecting any armistice, sister Canny," Amber said, "but the Felly are far too independent to do anything similar, and you'll surely find your outposts under siege the moment the Felly homeworld is freed of its embargo, even in the face of reason."

Kathy nodded, glad Amber had named the hurdle. "So we have strong motivation to remain united. The past twenty-five years of peace have been prosperous for the Canny."

"But not so for other races," Chabi said. "The Sylvy have suffered horribly!"

"They're hunted down, captured, and put to work in factories," Theresa added. "Those who remain free hide in caves, their burrows deep underground like rabbits!"

"They *are* rabbits," Chabi reminded her.

"They are? I was wondering how they managed to look so cuddly and cute." The Equy giggled.

"One of many races who remain oppressed," Kathy said. "A result that Professor Auigar predicted would result from Father's ambition. Another result that the Processor didn't predict was our current predicament—an interregnum in which an upstart has seized power."

Kathy took a chair beside Amber's, and gestured Theresa over, extending a hand to them both. Their hands linked, Kathy looked at them both. "I don't see these Terrans accepting our Regency any more than they did the Prime Minister's, and I know they'll outright reject any of us inheriting the throne directly, but we three are the only chance that our younger brother has to survive his minority. Cyrbodan Occuday is one of many who would usurp power and aver to hold it in trust until his Majesty the Heir Kublai Khan reaches his majority. Anyone would struggle with his or her cupidity to relinquish that power to the rightful heir, leading to strife, whether articulated in the subversive ways of stealth or poison, or in overt war.

"But what they will accept"—Kathy looked toward the three Terrans—"is a triumvirate of people formerly associated with his Majesty Chingis Khan, whose regency is enforced by the elder sisters of the Heir."

"I don't deserve to be entrusted with such august responsibility," Chabi said, her gaze in her lap.

"Of course you do," Mengu said.

"Your deep remorse declares to all your commitment to a just rule," Bati said. "If anyone's integrity might be questioned, it is surely mine for all the pirating I did along the outer reaches of the Empire."

"Why do you think his Highness sent my transpod to you, Chabi," Theresa said, "if not to summon you back to Earth to help rule his son's stead? What did you tell me? All to a purpose of his design, always by his design."

Chabi looked up, glancing at her male colleagues. "Would you want my help?"

"Want it? How could we do without it?"

Kathy smiled and stood. "I think we're agreed. Yes, being conquered was horrible, but breaking apart the Empire will engender worse. Humans won't let anyone but humans rule, so we rule them with a trio until his Majesty the Heir Kublai Khan comes of age."

"What about Occuday?"

Kathy looked among them. "Yes, what about Occuday?"

* * *

"I hope this works," Theresa said, throwing a glance at Chabi and Pilar.

They hovered above Earth in their transpod, Amber and her companions in their transpod beside them, Kathy on the other side with her Terran and Murry companions in hers.

Below, a hundred thousand conventional transpods—identical to the ones in which the three half-sisters had been summoned to Earth—stood ranked in the upper atmosphere of the Terran homeworld, as though poised to defend it against invasion.

Isn't that what we're doing? Invading? Theresa wondered, keeping the thought to herself.

Somewhere behind the phalanx of transpods was their target, the Prime Minister Cyrbodan Occuday, who had usurped the Regency and who would surely see that the heir Kublai Khan never reached the age to rule.

"When is a rebellion not a rebellion?" Bati had asked their group when they had first gathered, all nine of them, in the same room. "When you win."

Theresa smiled. This isn't a rebellion, because we're going to win.

"Time, distance, and mass," Kathy said. "We each take one dimension. Transpod technology prevents us from occupying the same interstitial field as already occupied by another transpod. That is the key to defeating Occuday."

Theresa grasped the controls, Pilar counting down with metronomic accuracy, just as Navid and Orozca were doing aboard the other two transpods.

"…Five, four, three, two…"

On zero, Theresa slammed her transpod into timelessness and dropped to Earth, keeping her eyes on the orange point of light on her porcelain disk, the location of Occuday's amulet, the shimmering transpod shell distorting their view.

The shock hurled them against their restraints.

"Incoming!" Theresa managed to say, and their transpod was pulverized by a fusillade of projectiles.

"The other transpods are bombarding us!" Chabi shouted, her voice barely audible over the explosions.

A vortex appeared ahead, their trajectory taking them right into it, a giant whirlpool into elsewhere.

"Reverse!" Pilar screamed.

Theresa slammed back on the controller, and their forward motion stopped.

A shadow occluded their view of the vortex, and the whirlpool disintegrated into a thousand pieces, the mini vortexes each dissipating quickly.

"That's Kathy!" Chabi said.

The orange dot on her amulet near, Theresa heard Pilar say, "… second phase, five, four, three …"

Theresa readied herself and on zero launched their transpod at Occuday's.

The Prime Minister's face splashed upon their vidscreen, then Amber's distorted face forcing itself in, and again when Kathy's squeezed onto it.

"You're surrounded, Occuday! There's no place else to go!"

"Unless I persuade you to release me," he leered. In his hands appeared the infant boy Kublai Khan. Occuday held a knife to his throat, the image twisting with interstitial perturbations.

Theresa gasped. Impasse!

"Slit his throat and you'll slit your own, Occuday," Bati's voice could be heard.

"Pirate scum! A fine Prime Minister you'd have made. You have a count of five!"

"One small wrinkle, Occuday," Chabi said.

"Scurrilous Schahahaday, what's it to you? You're an empty old bag of wind, of no more use to the Human race than a speck of dust to the galaxy. You bore me so! Five, four, three—"

"This is being viewed by subjects throughout the Empire," Chabi said. "You've cooked your own goose already, Occuday."

The surprise in his eyes was the signal.

Theresa slammed time into reverse, and the multi-verse collision rended reality across all three components of time, matter, and distance.

The rift in reality split beneath them, and they all hurtled into the abyss.

* * *

"I was wondering when you'd join me," the tall, handsome Terran male said, holding an infant boy in his arms, an ethereal light surrounding him, his cape held closed by a clasp that had once held an amulet.

Amber blinked at Chingis Khan. "I thought you were dead."

"Oh, I am, and intend to remain that way. My time is done, but yours has just begun. You and your siblings must return to your universe to complete the work that you're intended to do. Here," he said, handing the infant child to Amber.

She peeked at the boy enfolded in a gossamer blanket

He gurgled at her and laughed, reaching for her whiskers. Around his neck on a chain was the amulet.

The Emperor's amulet.

"Now go, my child, my daughter. As my youngest with eight more lives ahead of you—although I dare say this may count as one, your having come to this exalted place—you will see to the changes that I had hoped to bring about, more autonomy for the vassal states, the profit of their labors going to them and not to Earth, the peace preserved and the races intermingling without reservation and without conflict."

Amber frowned. "And what about you?"

"I'll watch from afar, much as my ancestor whose name I took watched his own empire grow and recede with the tides of time. My place is here, Amber Calico, and your place is there, with your sisters Kathy Mongrel and Theresa Appaloosa, guarding your brother who will one day become a greater Emperor than I could ever be, for he'll have the guidance of three older sisters.

"And when your last life has ended, you'll join me here, the universe a better place for your having lived your lives, all nine to them, to the best of your ability, which is considerable."

"Thank you, Father," she said, a tear slipping from her eye. "What shall I tell them?" Amber asked, jerking her thumb over her shoulder.

"About me?" Chingis Khan shook his head. "Nothing more than the truth—that I was a simple Terran with a larger vision than any person could hope to accomplish. But what's important isn't that I failed, is it?"

"No," Amber said, knowing already. "What's important is that you tried."

About the Author

Scott Michael Decker, MSW, is an author by avocation and a social worker by trade. He is the author of twenty-plus novels in the Science Fiction and Fantasy genres, dabbling among the sub-genres of space opera, biopunk, spy-fi, and sword and sorcery. His biggest fantasy is wishing he were published. His fifteen years of experience working with high-risk populations is relieved only by his incisive humor. Formerly interested in engineering, he's now tilting at the windmills he once aspired to build. Asked about the MSW after his name, the author is adamant it stands for Masters in Social Work, and not "Municipal Solid Waste," which he spreads pretty thick as well. His favorite quote goes, "Scott is a social work novelist, who never had time for a life" (apologies to Billy Joel). He lives and dreams happily with his wife near Sacramento, California.

Where to Find/How to Contact the Author

Websites:

- http://ScottMichaelDecker.com/
- http://www.linkedin.com/pub/scott-michael-decker/5b/b68/437
- https://twitter.com/smdmsw
- https://www.facebook.com/AuthorSmdMsw
- http://www.wattpad.com/user/Smdmsw

Lightning Source UK Ltd.
Milton Keynes UK
UKHW021059021120
372650UK00004B/713